ONE GOLD KNOT

DOMINANT CORD, BOOK 2

SADIE HALLER

QTP

ISBN-13: 978-0993826443

ISBN-10: 099382644X

ABOUT THIS BOOK

She didn't do relationships. She didn't even do all night.

After years of avoiding her teenage crush, Hildy Klein is shocked to come face to face with Wilson Kennedy.

Her uncle's wake isn't the place to unravel all the ways that Wilson could leave her emotionally vulnerable and exposed, yet his gentle persistence is impossible to ignore.

But Wilson is no longer that boy in her fantasies, and now Hildy must decide if she will give up control and commit to the protective, kinky Dom he's become.

~ Books by Sadie Haller ~
Dominant Cord
One Gold Heart
One Gold Knot
One Gold Triquetra

Tainted Pearl
Tainted Pearl
Tainted Shadow

Frisky Beavers
Prime Minister
Dr. Bad Boy
Full Mountie
Mr. Hat Trick (coming 2017)

For my sweet, wonderful sister, J.
You are everything I aspire to be.

ONE

Wilson did a double take at the sign on the back of the Smart Car parked in front of The Squeaky Wheel, not sure he'd read it right. He turned to Sully and raised a brow. "Newly Dead?"

Sully chuckled. "Erich's instructions for his wake were frustratingly detailed."

They stomped the snow from their feet and entered the pub. Wilson immediately spotted the other members of their wind quintet, Dominant Cord, at the bar. He snagged Sully's sleeve and gently pulled him along as he went to join the group.

"Hey guys, we finally made it."

"Hi Wil, I was getting a little concerned," Finn said.

"Blame Sully. I had to drive like my grandmother because our delicate flower bitched and complained about his sore ribs."

Mac snorted and rolled her eyes. "Good grief, Sully. I don't know how you're supposed to be ready to play the upcoming concerts if you can't even handle a car-ride without whining."

"Geez, what does it take for a guy to get a little sympathy?"

"You could stop letting your cock make your dating decisions."

"Well, I'd never been ice-skating before, and it sounded like fun—"

Shaking her head in obvious disbelief, Mac interrupted. "Bullshit, Sully. You just wanted to touch her feet. Too bad you broke your ribs before you had the chance to be the perfect gentleman and help remove her skates."

Wilson lost interest in the conversation. While banter between Mac and Sully was generally entertaining, he was fed up with hearing about Sully's injury. He let his eyes wander, and the lone woman in the back corner of the room caught his attention. Hildy. He'd only met her that one time, years ago, but she snuck into his dreams with disturbing regularity. Her demeanour screamed stay away, but her haunted look made him want to scoop her into his arms and comfort her. "I'll be back later."

Griff followed his gaze and said, "Yeah, good luck with that."

Wilson crossed the floor, never once taking his eyes off his quarry.

THE MOMENT WILSON turned from the bar and caught her eye, Hildy was positive the universe was a sadistic asshole.

When he'd walked in with Sully earlier, her stomach hit

the floor and her heart raced so fast she thought she might black out. She couldn't believe her good fortune when he'd headed straight to the bar without so much as a side-ways glance.

Deep down, she knew he'd come, no matter how hard she tried to convince herself otherwise. It was bad enough she had to be here and say goodbye to the one person in her family who loved her — she didn't need her teenage crush bearing witness to her all-consuming grief, too.

Her only option now was to gain the upper-hand and get rid of him. She looked him in the eye. "Hello Wilson. Is there something I can help you with?"

"Hey, Hildy," he smiled and offered his hand, "it's been a long time, I didn't think you'd remember me."

Remember? How could she forget? That day was branded on her soul. Every night since then, she imagined she was swaddled in his arms instead of her blanket. And she always fucked with her eyes closed so she could pretend Wil was the one she was with.

Her mind drifted back to her fifteen year old self. Back then, she practised on her uncle's piano because her parents had sold hers when she stopped being their performing monkey. They'd been livid when she'd stood before that capacity crowd and made her apologies as she announced her immediate retirement.

She stamped down her outrage and forced her thoughts back to the day she met Wilson. Normally, she was long gone before students arrived for their lessons, but she'd been learning a new piece and was oblivious to her surroundings until her uncle placed a gentle hand on her shoulder.

Hildy nodded. "Yeah, I remember. My uncle cajoled

me into accompanying you, and afterwards, you walked me to the library." That wasn't all he'd done that afternoon. He'd touched her, held her, oh, and he'd kissed her. She'd been emotionally ill-equipped to handle the unfamiliar feelings, and she'd successfully avoided further contact with him. Until now.

"That's right." Wilson's smile morphed into that irresistible lop-sided grin. He paused, his eyes swept across the empty table top and then back to her face. "How about I grab us a drink and we can catch up?"

Hildy silently cursed temptation and lied. "If you don't mind, I'd prefer to be on my own."

Wilson lifted an eyebrow. "Are you positive?"

From the corner of her eye Hildy saw the elderly couple walk in. Fuck. Georg and Martha. The universe was definitely not on her side today. They headed straight for her and she needed Wilson gone. Now. She'd survived a lot over the years, but she couldn't handle being humiliated by them in front of the only guy she'd ever met who could matter. "Absolutely. Now, if you don't mind...?"

To her horror, he pulled out the chair next her and sat. Then it was too late. They stood before her, and she couldn't do anything but ride out the oncoming shit-storm.

"Brunehilde." She could hear the sneer in his voice, and she tried not to cringe at the use of her full name. "I should have known you'd show up where you're not welcome. But then, you never were a smart girl, so I'll spell it out for you in short, simple words. Get the fuck out, you selfish cunt." Hildy stared blankly at the wall and mentally assumed the fetal position, prepared for the rest of Georg's tirade.

"That's enough. Nobody speaks to Hildy like that. Go

find somewhere else to spew your toxic feculence." It was Wilson's dangerously quiet voice that yanked Hildy from her safe place. She looked over to see her uninvited guest had risen to his feet, towering over the couple as he upbraided them.

"How dare you," Martha sputtered, "is that how you were taught to speak to your elders?"

"No, this is how I was taught to stick up for someone who is being bullied. Age, gender, and relationship are irrelevant."

Hildy could barely keep her jaw off the floor. The only person who ever effectively stood up to them in her defence was dead.

"Well, I never. I don't need to stand here and be insulted like this. Come on Georg, let's go find somewhere to sit." Martha dragged Georg with her as she stalked off towards an empty table.

Sully arrived moments later. "I'm sorry, sweetie, I got side-tracked. Are you okay? They weren't invited, but I should have known they'd show up anyway."

"I'm fine." Hildy angled her head towards Wilson. "Besides, your buddy here delivered a most righteous smack-down."

Sully grinned. "Damn, and I missed it."

"Yes, you did. I might fill you in on the all the juicy details over dinner one night this week, if you're buying." Hildy batted her eyelashes and shot Sully a cheeky smile.

"Deal. Now, I've got to get this show on the road." Sully leaned in to give Hildy a kiss on the cheek and whispered, "I know you need some space, but let him stay, sweets. Trust me."

"I'll consider it."

"Good enough. You're up first. I figured you'd prefer to get it all done and out of the way."

After all these years, she shouldn't be surprised at his ability to anticipate her needs. Her uncle taught him well. She choked back her tears. "Thank you."

As he was leaving, Sully pointed to Wilson and said, "Trust. Me."

Wilson's gentle touch on her shoulder felt nice in a way that still scared her. "Hildy, what can I do?"

Dammit, she needed him to go away. "Look, I appreciate you sticking up for me, but I can take care of myself. Now, if you don't mind, I really do want to be left alone"

"Hildy, whether you realise it or not, what you want is not necessarily what you need. I'll sit here quietly and you can pretend to be alone if you like, but you need a buffer."

"Why do men always think they know what's best for me?"

"Honey, I just watched you disappear inside yourself. I wouldn't leave anyone open to more of that kind of abuse. It's clear you're hurting, and I only want to give you a safe environment in which to cope. Can you let me do that?"

She was torn, but her intense urge to run home and bundle up in her blanket was eclipsed by love and respect for her uncle. She had come emotionally prepared to deal with Georg and Martha, but this handsome, kind, annoying man had thrown her off, and now she felt vulnerable. Wilson's voice interrupted her inner turmoil.

"Stop, you're going to give yourself an aneurysm. Just breathe. I'm going to get you some water, but before I leave, I'm going to give you a quick kiss on the lips because I think an implied relationship might help keep those asshats at bay."

Hildy didn't have time to respond before his lips grazed her own. All those lonely nights she lay awake remembering the feel of his kisses did nothing to prepare her for the riot this one incited between her thighs. It was the first good feeling she'd had in days. She stole glance at Martha and Georg, and took some perverse pleasure at their indignant scowls. Maybe company wasn't a bad idea. Besides, he was still awfully pretty to look at, and maybe she'd score another kiss or two. She wished she could take him home for a good fuck, but he was her long-time crush and she didn't do relationships. Hell, she didn't even do all night, and she was willing to bet he did both.

"Here you go."

Hildy snapped out of her daydream and managed a small smile for Wilson as he set the water in front of her. "Thank you."

He trailed a finger down her cheek. "You're welcome."

His small gesture created a big wet spot in her panties and an even bigger lump in her belly. She didn't know how to process touching like this. Too scary. A kiss would have been better. She could handle kissing. Fuck, company was such a bad idea. "You haven't asked me who they are."

"No, I haven't. Like everything else, you'll tell me when you're ready. Now, hush. I promised to just sit here and let you be."

Ready? She was never ready, but she'd opened the door, and it was time to shove Wilson through it. "Not your typical meet the parents, was it?"

"Your parents? Are you fucking shitting me?"

Hildy cringed slightly before straightening and lifting her chin. "I wish I were, but there it is. I didn't even rate a booby prize in the parent lottery."

"I guess not, and I'm sorry for that." Wilson cupped her cheek and leaned in for another kiss. "It looks like things are going to get started soon. Is there anything you need before it gets crazy?"

What the fuck? People couldn't dump her fast enough after meeting her parents. This was one man Hildy did not know how to handle. He said and did all the right things. How could he possibly know what she needed when she didn't even know herself?

"No, thank you. My uncle asked me to come out of retirement and perform tonight, just for him. It's been a long time since I've had an audience, so, I'm going to need a few minutes to myself to get my head screwed on straight."

"Whatever you need."

Hildy took some deep breaths in an effort to calm down. Damn Uncle Erich anyway for making her promise to do this. Why did he have to get sick and die? Life was so fucking unfair. She didn't realise she was crying until she felt the tears being wiped from her face. She looked at Wilson and tried to smile.

"It's okay, sweetie, you go ahead and let it out."

"Later. I'll let it out later. I really do need to get my shit together. The worst thing I can do is fuck this up with my parents right there."

Wilson stroked her cheek as he gazed into her eyes. "What's your favourite colour?"

"What?"

He winked and shot her that sexy lopsided grin of his. "Work with me here."

Against her better judgement, Hildy gave in and played along. "Dark purple, what's yours?"

"That pretty shade of hazel I see when I look into your eyes."

"Feeding me lines of bullshit is not helpful."

"Sweetheart, I don't bullshit. Ever. Favourite thing to have for supper?"

"Hmmm," Hildy tapped her chin as she considered, "chicken sandwiches with mayonnaise and cranberry sauce."

Wilson laughed. "That's lunch."

"It's whatever I want it to be. So there." Hildy grinned and stuck her tongue out.

"You're awfully cheeky. If you were mine, there might be consequences for display like that."

"Well, I'm not yours." Hildy paused, then curiosity got the better of her. "But if I were, what kind of consequences?"

"Oh honey, this is not the kind of conversation I had in mind. Not yet, anyway."

Hildy had known Sully her whole life; she knew precisely what sorts of shenanigans his quintet got up to in Finn's basement, and she had a pretty good idea what Wilson meant by consequences. Surprisingly, she found the prospect arousing, but Wil was right about this not being where her head should be right now. She squeezed her legs together and tried not to squirm, but that wet spot in her panties kept growing.

Her focus shifted as Sully's voice drifted through the sound system. "May I have your attention, everyone." Once the room was silent, he continued, "We're here to celebrate the life of Erich Klein. I know most of you were unaware of his illness, and his death came as a shock. That's how he wanted it. Shortly before he died, Erich sat me down and gave me a long list of orders to be executed upon his death and threatened to haunt me silly if I didn't. Needless to say, the miserable bugger has kept me hopping from the moment he kicked the bucket.

"As you can see," Sully pointed at the glass box on the bar, "I've burnt the body, but only because I couldn't convince the undertaker to embalm him with good single malt scotch. Make sure you have a drink with him and tell him a funny story.

"Erich had three absolute loves in his life. Ted, music, and Hildy. He lost Ted in their third year of university, back when gay-bashing wasn't a hate-crime. With Ted gone, he buried himself in the deepest part of the closet, music his only joy. Then Hildy came along and filled the hole in his heart.

"At Erich's request, Hildy has agreed to perform *Gounod's Funeral March of a Marionette*. For the non-music geeks here today, you may recognise it as the theme music from the TV show, *Alfred Hitchcock Presents*."

Hildy had known this moment was coming for days, but she still felt woefully unprepared. As she stood, Wilson took her hand and kissed her knuckles. "You'll be fine sweetheart. I'll be right here when you're done."

Hildy forced herself towards the piano. Her heart was broken, but her uncle didn't want her to be sad. She thought back to all his other seemingly impossible edicts, and almost smiled. As she reached the performance area, Sully gave her a gentle hug and whispered, "It'll be fine. He loved you. Now give him everything you've got."

Before settling at the piano, Hildy looked up into Sully's watery eyes. "Thanks."

As soon as she played the first notes, the people and the

room no longer existed for her. There was only the piano, and the music. The tightness in her chest eased, and she felt just a little less sad. Her uncle had an uncanny ability to give her what she needed. Even in death.

WILSON WATCHED as Hildy poured herself into the music. He thought back to the unforgivable way her parents treated her. He stole a glance at the couple in question and wasn't surprised to see them sporting identical scowls. Fuck 'em.

He was glad he'd made that split-second decision to shield Hildy from that noxious pair of wank-stains, and he didn't consider it a hardship to continue. That glint in her eye when she asked him about consequences was promising. He wasn't opposed to a little funishment. Damn. Her long legs and luscious lips had him more than interested, but the way she caressed that piano made him wish his cock were the ivory beneath her fingers. No doubt every other man in the room had similar thoughts.

With the decay of the final note, Wilson hurried to meet Hildy and escort her back to their table. His drive to protect her was strong, but the broken look on her face during the incident with her parents had him almost feral.

Sully thanked Hildy, and Wilson gathered her close, planting a kiss the top of her head. "That was beautiful, love." He kept his arm around her as he guided her along. Before she could take her seat, he parked himself on his own and pulled her onto his lap. He was quick to wrap his arms around her and tuck her head beneath his chin. He breathed easy once he felt her body relax. "There you go, sweetheart, just rest." With a nod of reassurance to Sully, Wilson hugged Hildy a little tighter and rocked her back and forth as she sobbed. "Let it out, love, I've got you, and I'll keep you safe."

Sully headed towards Wilson and Hildy as soon as he finished introducing the next performance. "Is she okay, Wil?"

"She will be. Right now she needs a cuddle and good cry."

"Agreed. Should I make other arrangements for getting home?"

"Nope, I'm a firm believer in leave with the one ya brung. That said, I think we'll be in charge of making sure Hildy gets home safely."

Hildy pulled her head back from Wilson's body. "I am perfectly capable of getting myself home safely, thank you very much."

Sully reached out and stroked her hair. "Nobody is saying otherwise, sweetheart, but it's been a difficult, emotional day, and unfortunately, it's likely to get worse before it gets better. I need you to trust me when I tell you it will get much, much better, but for now, let us support you, okay?"

With a long sigh, Hildy gave in. "Okay. I'm too wrung out to argue."

"Promise?"

"I promise."

"Good girl. Wil, I have to go up there and do more official stuff..."

"No worries, I've got her back. One thing, though. Can you give Mac a heads-up on the situation? I don't want

Hildy to be alone anywhere, and I can't be with her if she needs the facilities."

"No need, she caught that little encounter with the cum infested pus bubbles and was all set to kick some ass. Your way was likely more elegant, but hers is always worth the price of admission."

"I'll die a happy man if I get through the rest of my life without feeling the sharp-side of her tongue."

"Good luck with that. Oops, that's my cue. Gotta go. Hildy, remember, Wilson is here to lean on, and you promised."

Hildy nodded and buried herself in Wilson's arms. He kissed the top of her head before resting his cheek there.

WILSON OPENED the front passenger door of his car. "In you get, Hildy. Sully can sit in the back."

"I don't mind taking the back seat. Sully's injured, so he should get the front."

"Not a chance, I had to put up with him in the front the whole way here. He's notorious for back-seat driving, so he may as well be appropriately located."

"I thought you liked me, Wilson," Sully complained.

"I do like you, but given the choice between a hot woman and you sitting next me, you're going to lose every single time."

Hildy's face flushed and she dropped her gaze to the ground.

"Now look what you did," Sully accused.

"It's fine, Sully, really. Stop fussing. One minute you act like Wilson is the best thing that could possibly happen to me, and the next you're behaving like he's an axe-murderer."

"You know me, I'm not happy unless I'm fussing."

"Well, yeah, but stop it." Hildy demanded.

"Get in the car. I hurt, and I want to go home."

"Oh god." Wilson turned to Hildy. "Do you mind if we drop Sully off first? I'd like to get home before dawn."

Hildy chuckled. "Nope, I'm all for self-preservation, and this will minimise how much complaining we both have to endure."

"Seriously? You too, Hildy?"

"Oh, suck it up, you big baby," Wilson ordered. "It's been almost six weeks since you broke those ribs. If you can't handle a ride in the car, how do you expect to be ready to play in time for all the Valentine's gigs?"

"I'll manage just fine as long as you don't add to the damage now."

"Oh for fuck's sake. Get in the back and be quiet or we'll visit every pot-hole and speed bump in the city before I drop you right back here and you can get a cab home." Wilson lifted his eyebrows. "Still want to bitch about my driving?"

Sully clamped his lips shut and slid into the back of the car.

Hildy sniggered. "Thanks, Wilson. I am SO making a special note of this. I don't think I've ever seen anyone shut Sully up so effectively without a ball-gag."

"Ball-gag? Tell me it's true and there is photographic evidence." Wilson glanced up at the rear-view mirror for Sully's reaction. Nothing. Damn him and that inscrutable face of his. He turned his head for a quick look at Hildy and not only knew she told the truth, but whip poker with her would be oodles of fun. "Well, is there?"

"No comment," Hildy said as she turned her face towards the passenger side window.

Wilson snuck another quick glance in the rear-view mirror, and was sure he saw a flash of relief in Sully's eyes. Interesting. This would be worth pursuing.

The ride to Sully's place was quiet and uneventful, but once Sully was safely indoors, that changed. Wilson drove a few blocks and parked the car. He turned to Hildy, and with a penetrating stare, he began his interrogation.

"You had to know I wouldn't let this one go, so I suggest you give in gracefully and tell me all there is to know about Sully wearing a ball-gag."

"I have nothing to tell you."

Wilson's eyes flashed. "That's complete bullshit. Let's get one thing straight, right now. You do not lie to me. Ever. Not even little tiny white ones meant to avoid hurt feelings. Are we clear?"

"You're in no position to make demands of me. In addition, Mr. Hypocrite, you sit there and tell me never to lie to you, but your implication of a relationship to keep Martha and Georg off my back sure smells like a lie to me."

"True, it was certainly a lie by implication, but I lied to a pair of bullies with whom I have no obligation of trust so I could protect a woman with whom I am interested in exploring a trusting relationship."

"Look, while I appreciate what you did to protect me, our implied relationship ended the moment we left the Squeaky Wheel. Now, if you don't mind, I'm tired and I'd like to go home."

"Regardless of whether we're romantically involved or not, we now have a relationship of a sort, and I will accept nothing less than the truth from you."

"Our relationship, whatever it may be, ends the moment I get out of this car, which will be here and now if we're not moving in the next ten seconds."

"Hold on..."

"Eight...seven..."

Wilson started the car and eased onto the road. "Can we at least talk whilst I'm driving?"

"No. I just want to get home. It's been a long, tedious day."

"Okay, quiet it is."

Wilson briefly considered taking the long way to Hildy's house in case she might be tempted to engage in some conversation, but if he were to have any chance with her, he needed to play it completely straight. Even in the silence, the ten minutes it took to get Hildy home sped by too quickly and left Wilson wanting more.

"Thanks for the ride."

"You're welcome, sweetheart." Wilson got out of the car along with Hildy.

"What are you doing?"

"Making sure you get home safely. Just go with it and let me be the gentleman my mother thinks she raised."

Hildy rolled her eyes and sped up the path to her house, Wilson keeping pace beside her. Once Hildy had the door open, Wilson placed his hands on her upper arms and gently turned her towards him. "Since our relationship is about to turn into a pumpkin, may I please have one last kiss?"

"Good grief, Wilson, will you give it up already?"

"I'm persistent. It's one of my many redeeming qualities."

"Oh, what the hell. One kiss."

Wilson gathered Hildy into his arms. He touched his lips to her forehead, her nose, and finally to her lips before trailing his tongue along the seam of her mouth. She opened to him and he deepened the kiss, tangling his tongue with hers in between teasing sucks and nips. When Wilson finally eased way from Hildy, he studied her face and smiled. She was just as affected. "What time shall I pick you up in the morning to get your car?"

"You don't need to do that. I can manage on my own."

"I won't leave you stranded for tomorrow. So, what time would you like me to pick you up in the morning?"

Hildy huffed. "Can you be here by eight-fifteen? I have a student at nine."

"I'll be here. Goodnight, sweetheart. Now, go inside and lock the door. I'm not moving from this spot until you do."

"You are awfully bossy."

"It comes with the territory. You'll get used to it."

"Cocky much?"

"Go."

"Alright, I'm going, I'm going."

Once he heard the deadbolt snick into place, Wilson returned to his car and headed home. He'd known she'd be at Erich's wake, but he hadn't been prepared for how intensely attracted he still was to her. He thought back to that afternoon when they were teenagers. He was pretty sure he'd been her first kiss. Damn, he'd wanted to be her first everything, but he never saw her again. He didn't need to be her first anymore, but he did want to be her only.

TWO

HILDY OPENED the door to a far too cheery looking Wilson. "Seriously? It's not even seven-thirty. Nobody has a right to look that happy this early in the morning. I'm sure we agreed you'd pick me up at eight-fifteen."

"While I am a trifle early, I do come bearing coffee and croissants."

She'd had a restless night and she wanted to stay irritated, but couldn't. "Actually, I slept though my alarm. Now I get to start my day with both breakfast and caffeine. Thank you."

"Does this mean I've earned a good morning kiss?"

"You are incorrigible."

"So my mother keeps telling me. I'm still waiting for my answer."

Hildy considered his request. His kisses tested her self-control to the limit, and last night she'd been on the verge of inviting him in. However, giving him quick peck on the lips should be okay. "Only if you let me drink my coffee in peace. I am not a morning person."

Wilson's ability to give her the quiet she needed to prepare herself for the day ahead was a relief. The very few men she'd woken up with had been incapable. Oh, they'd be quiet for a minute or two when she asked them, but they couldn't handle the silence. She wondered how long Wilson could hold out. He'd surprised her the previous evening when he'd complied with her request for a quiet journey home, but that was only ten minutes.

Then she realised he wouldn't ask about Sully and the ball-gags as long as he was being quiet. If she could keep this up until she got to her car, she'd be off the hook. No looking for ways to tell the truth without giving anything away. She picked off pieces of the croissant and slipped them into her mouth between sips of coffee. Then it hit her. He knew how she took it. Sully was such a blabber-mouth. She finished her breakfast and drained her cup.

"Right, I need to jump in the shower and throw some clothes on, then I'll be ready to go." Hildy leaned in and gave Wilson the kiss he'd earned. Damn, he made her tingle all over. She pulled away quickly, he was far too tempting.

WILSON REMAINED silent for the short journey back to the Squeaky Wheel. Hildy needed space. He could give her that, and it allowed him time to consider her other needs. His long conversation with Sully the previous night had given him a better idea of who Hildy was, but even Sully, who knew her best, was not privy to all that made her tick.

"Thanks for the ride, I appreciate it."

"You're most welcome. I'm sure I'll see you around."

"Yeah, maybe, but don't count on it."

"Would you like to bet on it?"

"Nope, the only luck I have is generally very bad. Now, I need to go or I'm going to be late."

"Alright, no betting. A kiss and hug goodbye?"

"No hug. Just a quick kiss." Hildy amended.

"A quick kiss, then. "Wilson's eyes never left hers as he took her face in his hands, and when their lips touched, he needed more. His instincts took over and he was lost. He wrapped his arms around her and tried to deepen the kiss, his tongue coaxing her to open for him.

He knew he'd screwed up the moment he'd done it, but by then, it was too late. Hildy yanked back and scrambled out of the car. She poked her head back in. "Silly me, I thought you might be different, but you really are a hypocrite. You agree to one thing and do another, just like most everyone else I've ever met. I don't ever want to see you again." She slammed the door and stalked to her car.

Wilson waited until she'd driven off before restarting his vehicle. He'd meant to return home, but instead, he ended up at Sully's.

HE LAUNCHED into his tale of woe the moment the door opened. "I fucked up, and now I need your help."

"You'd best come in, then." Sully stepped aside and allowed Wilson to pass, then followed him into the kitchen. He poured them each a cup of coffee and joined Wil at the table. A long sip later, he asked, "What did you do?" Sully remained silent until Wil finished telling him of his morning encounter with Hildy.

"Fuck, fuck, fuck. Goddammit, Wil. You're the epitome of patience, and never impulsive. I warned you last night to tread very, very carefully. She let you touch and hold her — something I've never seen her let anyone do besides Erich and me. I thought you might actually be someone with whom she could feel safe enough with to involve herself romantically."

"I have no excuse. That rocket clearly exploded before lift-off, so now I need to fix this for both of us."

"I don't know, Wil. Your fuck-up pretty much squandered my credibility. I told her she could trust you and you made a liar out of me." Sully closed his eyes and tapped his chin with his forefinger. "Give me a few days to see what I can do. In the meantime, stay away from her and don't come over here without calling first."

He was so ridiculously desperate, he'd have agreed to perform their next concert wearing nothing but a cock-ring. "Okay."

"Good boy."

"That's hilarious coming from a Dom whose mouth is, apparently, no stranger to a ball-gag."

Sully's expression gave nothing away. "Pure speculation on your part."

"Maybe, but I don't think so."

"Whatever. Now, fuck off, I've got to go slip into my superhero persona. I have relationships to rescue."

Wilson snorted. "Superhero! Dream on, Sully."

"I still owe Mac two favours to be named later. If I pull this off, they become your responsibility."

"Deal. Keep me updated. It's going to kill me sitting at home wondering what's going on."

"Yes, yes. Now, piss off, I have plans to make."

Wilson got up to leave and paused. "I'm sorry I fucked up, Sully. If nothing else, I hope you can salvage your relationship with Hildy."

"She and I have been friends her whole life, I doubt she'll ditch my ass over this. However, she will probably make me suffer for a bit, and that's okay, I'll take it out on you." Wilson nodded and left.

HILDY STARED at the ringing phone. She was tempted to let it go to voice-mail, but she knew he'd just keep calling until she answered.

"Hello, Sully, you rat-bastard. You're lucky I bothered to answer." She flopped onto the sofa and put her feet up on the coffee table.

"Well, I'm glad you did. I have some business that requires your attention. Can you swing by tonight?"

"Can't we do it over the phone?"

"No, there's paperwork and signatures involved. Besides, I can start atoning for my sins by providing you with a yummy supper."

"Pizza from Cheeses Crust?"

"Is there anywhere else?"

"Just you and me?"

"If by just you and me, you mean no Wilson, then yes, just us. I made him promise to stay away. Good enough?"

"I can live with that."

"Thank you. Can we talk about what happened today?"

Hildy groaned. "Do we have to?"

"No, but I feel responsible. I shouldn't have trusted anyone else with your safety."

Sometimes, he really was an over-protective dolt. "You buffoon, safety wasn't the issue. Trust was the issue, and while Wilson had managed to earn a little, he pissed it away in the space of a heartbeat."

"And he knew it the very moment he did it. With most people, I wouldn't bother advocating a second chance, but I've known him a very long time. I have seen him at both his strongest, and his most vulnerable. This is the first time I've known him to be impulsive. That tells me that there's something about you that short-circuited his rigid self-control."

And there he was, back to meddlesome. "Stop right there, Sully. I wasn't interested in him before he proved himself a hypocrite, so why would I open myself up to him now?"

"I'm not suggesting you marry the guy, or even date him. Just give him a chance to show you he's a pretty good guy who sometimes makes mistakes, but will always do everything he can to fix them."

"To be honest, Sully, I wasn't going to ever see him again regardless of whether he fucked-up or not. I'll admit to a bit of an interesting spark. But I'm smart enough to know it is nothing more than an emotional reaction to grief combined with the knight in shining armour routine he pulled when my parents showed up. Sleep took care of that."

"Okay, I won't push for you to socialise with him, but will you let him get his trustworthiness back to zero?"

"He did save my ass this morning. You told him to

show up with breakfast and coffee, didn't you?" Hildy wondered why Sully was pushing this so hard.

"Busted. I gave Finn help when it came to Mac, so it was only fair to give Wil a little guidance on navigating the maze that is Hildy Klein."

"You are nothing but a hopeless romantic. How about you stop trying to make matches for your friends and work a little harder on one for yourself. It's time you stop being a man-slut and settle down with a nice little switch."

"You didn't say anything to Wilson about my occasional side-trips to the ouchy end of the hitty-stick, did you?"

"Of course not. Nobody's business but yours. I'm sorry I let that bit about the ball-gag slip out last night."

"Ah, the truth comes out. You're drowning in guilt for almost outing me. I thought your forgiveness was a little too easily won. A word of warning, sweetie, you'll need to be on your guard with Wil over your little slip. He brought it up with me today, so he's not going to let it go."

"You know, Sully, if you'd just come clean with the group, neither of us would have to watch our mouths. What's the big deal?"

"Dominant Cord. That doesn't exactly scream four Doms and a switch, does it?"

Hildy let out a long, exasperated breath. "You are such an idiot. You said it yourself, occasional trips. That doesn't make you less of a Dom. What's with the identity crisis?"

"I don't know. Maybe it's because I haven't played in weeks, and these broken ribs make me feel less-than."

"Whiner. Hurry up and get healed so you can pick up a hitty-stick and strike terror in the backsides of subbies everywhere."

"Are you sure you're not kinky?"

"Nope, not a bit. What time's supper?"

"I'll order for about six, but how about you be here for five so we can go through the paperwork first, then relax."

"There really is paperwork? I thought you were making up a reason for me to come over."

"While I did want you to come over, I was not going to fuck up by giving you a bullshit story. You're Erich's sole beneficiary, and there is a whole bunch of paperwork I need to go through with you. I'll see you later."

"See ya." Hildy disconnected the call and set her phone down on the sofa. She thought back to Sully's question about being kinky. Her answer was automatic, but no longer fully honest. Great, she'd flat-out lied to Sully. Another thing to feel guilty over. Sully'd been regularly asking her that same question for so many years, the answer was out before she'd taken last night's conversation with Wilson into account.

Consequences. Before Wil had brought the subject up, she hadn't felt more than mild curiosity about the sorts of activities Sully and his friends engaged in. But as soon as Wil had said mine, and consequences, she was done for.

As much as she wanted to pretend she hadn't developed an interest in the kinky side of life, she knew she'd have to come clean with Sully. He'd been telling her for years she'd change her tune one day. It was just her luck one day happened to be at her uncle's funeral. She glanced at the clock, plenty of time to have a long, hot soak in the tub. Her week had gone to shit in a handbag when Sully told her of her uncle's death, and that handbag had to have the interior proportions of a TARDIS, because the shit just kept on coming.

Hildy twisted the taps on the tub, and after a couple of minutes checked the temperature with her hand. Cold. She turned off the cold, and on discovering there was no hot water, she was ready to give up and go to bed. She was tempted to call Sully and cancel, but if she gave her inability to bathe as an excuse, he'd just tell her to come early and bathe there. Aw hell, she wanted a nice hot bath, and considering the big gift of 'I told you so' she was about to bestow upon him, the least Sully could do was supply her with a tub full of hot water for a couple of hours. She shut off the faucet and went in search of her phone.

"ARE YOU EVER COMING OUT? You take the most epic baths of anyone I've ever known."

Hildy groaned, marked her place, and set her book on the closed lid of the toilet. "I'll be down in fifteen minutes, now leave me be."

"Hurry up, I'm tired of having a naked woman in my house and not being able to play with her."

Maybe she was right to wait until after her bath to give him his 'I told you so' moment. While she trusted him completely, she was sure her handbag had room for more shit, and she was not about to hold it open.

She pulled the plug and stood, letting the water slide off her body and into the tub before grabbing one of Sully's thick, fluffy towels. She loved these towels. In most things, Sully was the classic, manly bachelor, but he did have the odd redeeming domestic quirk, and a closet full of plush towels was one of them. She threw on her clothes and headed down to 'fess up to Sully."

"Hey gorgeous. Feel better?"

"A little."

"Aw, sweetie, come sit down. What's wrong?"

There was no holding back; her confession gushed from her lips. "I lied to you. When I said I had no interest in kink, I lied. There's really no excuse for it, but it had been the truth for so long, when you asked the usual question, I gave you my usual answer and once it was out, I didn't know what to do..."

Sully finished for her. "But the guilt was eating you alive, and you just had to own up. Sweetie, thanks for your honesty. Truth is, I ask that question more because I liked to fluster you than out of self-interest. If I were a proper gentleman, I'd leave it there, but I'm a nosy busy-body. When did it change?"

"Believe it or not, last night."

Sully's eyes twinkled. "Wilson did get to you, then?"

"He did, but what I said about not wanting to see him again was true."

"A one-eighty like that is bound to scare the beejeezus out of you, and the last thing I can imagine you'd want to do is spend time with someone who has such a profound effect on your sexuality."

"Fuck, Sully, sometimes I swear you're psychic, or something."

"Not even close. I'd say it has more to do with knowing you since we were kids. So, what happened last night that changed your mind about kink?"

"Something Wilson said."

"And..." Sully prompted.

"Damn you, Sully. Are you really going to make me tell you everything?"

"Of course I am. So, spill."

Hildy huffed. "Okay, fine. He said something to the effect of 'if you were really mine, there'd be consequences.' Can we drop it now?"

"Hell, no. What on earth did you do that had the potential to earn you a visit from Wil's rather inventive side?"

"I was a bit cheeky and stuck my tongue out."

Sully nodded sagely. "A word of caution. Unless your tongue is doing delicious things to drive Wilson wild, you may want to keep it safely in your mouth. I am not kidding when I say, he has some pretty effective ways of dealing with cheeky subs who stick their tongues out inappropriately."

"Oh, please. It's safe to say it will never be a problem because I'll never be his."

"Sweetie, I don't know what I want more, for you to be right, or to eat your words. Both options have merit."

"Contrary to your self-important belief, it's not about you. Shouldn't our supper be here by now?"

THREE

Hildy gathered the mess of envelopes from the floor below the letter-slot and sifted through them. Mostly junk and bills, but one caught her eye. She checked the return address and briefly considered returning it to the sender. Curiosity won out. She set her morning coffee on the table and slipped her finger beneath the flap, sliding it in one smooth motion from one side to the other. She reached in with her thumb and forefinger and extracted the contents, a folded slip of paper and an old photo of her uncle playing his clarinet.

She smiled. His stance and expression were familiar, the photo was not. She spent a few minutes studying the image, making a mental note to get it framed. Finally, she unfolded the paper and read:

Dear Hildy,
I thought you'd like to have this one.
Wilson

She reread the words and smiled. It screamed Sully and his inability to keep his meddling nose out of anyone's business. She had a call to make.

"You meddlesome old fart."

"Ah the dulcet tones of my favourite piano teacher," Sully replied.

"You coached him. You gave him that photograph to send, didn't you?"

"Calm down. What are you talking about? What photograph?"

"The one of Uncle Erich."

"Sorry sweetie, I don't know what you're talking about."

"Damn."

"What's the matter?"

"I was hoping it was another one of your sneaky ploys so I could use it to justify not forgiving him."

"Why would you need to justify it? Either you do, or you don't. It's not a judgement thing."

"Damn you Sully. I hate that you know me so fucking well."

"Yes, I do, and how many times has it been to your advantage?"

"Way more than I care to admit."

"He's really got your emotions tied in knots, hasn't he?"

"Unfortunately, yes."

"I suspect that's not all he'll have tied in knots before too long."

"What's that supposed to mean?" She asked, already knowing the answer.

"One step at a time. You're interested in the kinky side of life, these days. How about you join me at Finn's next play party. I won't be up for playing, so it would give you a good, safe opportunity to see what it's about. You'll be able to watch and ask all the questions you like."

Seriously? He was expecting her to jump in with both feet and go to a fucking kink-fest? "I don't know, Sully. I don't know if I'm ready for that kind of thing."

"The next party isn't for another week, so no need to decide right away. How about I email you links to some websites with good, accurate information so you can do a little research, okay? If left to your own devices, I shudder to think what kind of freakiness you could stumble upon and scare you away before you even get started."

"I'd appreciate that, Sully. I'll admit to giving in to my curiosity a time or two. I've even gone so far as to do a search, but I've never actually had the nerve to click on any links. The little thumbnails that showed up sent me scurrying for the back-button every single time." Boy had they ever. But they stopped her from wondering.

"Wow, I never thought you had even enough curiosity to type in a search. I guess I don't know you quite as well as I like to think I do."

"Score one for me. I never thought I would see the day where you weren't at least one step ahead of me. Look, I'm going to go. I have some thinking to do."

"I imagine you do. Give me an hour and there'll be an email bursting with kinky-linky goodness in your inbox."

"Thanks, Sully. I'll catch you later."

"So long, Sweets."

It had been days since he'd gone to Sully for help, and

Wil's patience was wearing thin. He hadn't heard anything from Hildy either, but he hadn't expected to. He'd have sent that photo regardless of whether they were in a committed relationship or sworn enemies. No strings attached. The ringing phone caught his attention. He took a quick look at the incoming number and smiled. Finally. "Sully, you have uncanny timing. I was just thinking of calling you."

"You're an idiot. I told you to stay the hell away from her. It's only dumb fucking luck your stunt didn't backfire."

Wil walked into the kitchen and poured himself a cup of coffee. "It wasn't a stunt, Sully. I was going through some stuff, reminiscing, and as soon as I saw it, I knew she had to have it."

"Luck was with you, that's for sure. That's not why I called."

"Oh, really?"

"I had a very interesting conversation with Hildy and I'm only sharing it with you because you are relevant to it as both subject, and potential ally."

"Sully, I know you look upon yourself as a kind of fixer, but sometimes, you need to let things work out in their own way."

"Not this time." Sully paused. "That conversation you and she had about ownership and consequences piqued her curiosity, and she's interested in exploring life on the kinky side."

"I'm not surprised. Her reaction was pretty obvious, even though she tried hard to hide it."

Sully cleared his throat. "Given you seem to be the one who woke her desire to explore, I think it makes sense for you to be her guide."

"I don't know. I'm not one for taking on neophytes, even under the most clinical of circumstances." Wil took a sip of coffee and set it on the table. "Yes, she intrigues me. So much so, I made a rookie mistake that not only could have been the absolute end for anything between Hildy and me, it could have caused irreparable damage to your relationship with her."

"Give me a little credit, Wil. I wouldn't be asking this of you if I thought there was any chance you could put my relationship with Hildy at risk. I've already laid some ground-work for you and got her started on the theory portion of her education. Once I'm satisfied she's ready, you'll take care of the practical side."

"I don't know about this, Sully."

"What's to know? You are attracted to each other, and I trust you. Either it works out, or it doesn't."

"Damn it, Sully. She could get hurt emotionally."

"Yeah, she could, but I doubt it. She was destroyed emotionally by her own parents and just lost one of only two people in her life to give her unconditional love. My opinion of you would have to be seriously fucked up for you to be capable of hurting her worse than that."

Wil sighed. "I concede to your superior stubbornness. I will give it a try, but I also need to be satisfied she's ready before we venture into any physical activities."

"I can work with that."

"You said you've got her started on the theoretical. Care to enlighten me on what you mean by that?"

"I sent her links to a bunch of really good websites to get her started. I've ordered her a bunch of books for her e-reader as well. Both fiction and non-fiction. The one thing I didn't do, was send her a check-list. I thought that should be entirely between the two of you."

"Sounds like a good start. Have you spoken with her about having me be her physical guide to all things kinky?"

"Not yet. I wanted to give her time with all the written material first. I expect that will whet her appetite enough to be open to the suggestion."

"You are a sneaky bugger, you know that?"

"I'm all about the big picture. Even if things don't work out between the two of you, I know your treatment of her will put her on the road to a functional, loving, lasting relationship. She deserves that."

"Everyone deserves that. Should I not be in contact with her until you think she's ready to move forward?"

"Actually, no. I'm hoping she'll be up for accompanying me to Finn and Mac's party."

Wil exploded. "What? Are you fucking nuts?"

"Quite probably. I have two ideas from which to choose. The first option is for you to attend with a sub and play as normal so Hildy can see you in action, which will hopefully allay any concerns. The second option is for you to go stag so you can pay close attention to her reactions to the activities around her."

"You wouldn't be injecting an element of jealousy in the first scenario would you?"

"Well, I don't suppose a few twinges of jealousy on her part could hurt too much."

"You are a manipulative son of a bitch, Dave Sullivan."

"True, but I have good reasons."

"I think they're better reasons when they don't involve me."

"So, option one, or option two for the play party?"

"None of the above. " Wil tried not to laugh as he proceeded to ruin his friend's plans. "I'll be doing some rope work on Mac, so that's the only place my attention will be. Besides, until you know Hildy is going to attend, I expect there are more pressing matters to handle."

"Good point. Check-list comes to mind. I think that will be the best way to introduce your role in this. Once she's finished with all the reading, I'll bring up the need for her to do a check-list and suggest she exchange with you because it would be completely squicky for her to exchange with me. This whole business is bordering on squicky for me as it is."

Hildy tapped the table with her nail as the phone on the other end continued to ring. Please don't go to voice mail.

"Hello?"

"Oh Mac, thank fuck."

"Um, who is this?"

"Shit, I'm sorry. It's Hildy Klein, Sully's friend? We met at Erich Klein's wake, and you said I could call you if I ever needed to talk."

"Oh yeah, hi Hildy. What's the matter?"

"I'm sorry to bother you, but I need someone to talk to, and Sully isn't an option." And wasn't that an understatement.

"Do you want to talk now, over the phone, or in person?"

"I think over the phone might be easier. At least you won't be able to see me blush."

"Phone it is. What's up?"

Hildy dragged her fingers through her hair. "Fuck, I don't even know where or how to start."

"Does this have anything to do with Wilson?"

"Sully and his big mouth are dead."

"Calm down, Sully never said a word. I was at your uncle's wake, remember." Mac chuckled a little. "I saw the sizzle between the two of you. Are you coming to the play party?"

"Aw bugger. I'm all new at this kinky thing. I mean really new, as in I had only vague ideas until Sully sent me all those links."

"So, you're new. We've all been new at some point."

"But, I don't know how to do any of this stuff, and what if I hate it?"

"That's what check-lists are for. Have you done one yet?"

"They've come up in some of my reading, but no, I haven't done one. It's not like I have someone to share it with."

"You don't need someone to share it with. It's a great exercise for you to gain understanding of your own sexuality. This whole thing is based on trust, and you need to trust yourself first. I'll warn you up front, if you are completely honest with yourself, some of your answers will shock, and even embarrass you. You'll be tempted to adjust your answers to be more in line with what you perceive as societal norms. Don't. You need to accept yourself and your needs. If you don't, you'll never be satisfied, and honey, there is a lot to be said for satisfaction."

Hildy was more curious than ever. "Where do I find one?"

"There are all kinds available, but I'll email you a copy of the one Finn and I used. It's the same one the rest of Dominant Cord uses, so should you get the opportunity to exchange lists with Wilson, you'll be ahead of the game. Fair warning, it's explicit and I don't think it leaves any kink or fetish unexplored."

"Thanks, Mac. I feel a little better now."

"Good. You still haven't told me if you're coming to the next play party."

"God, no. I don't even know if I could do this in private. How could I possibly do it in public?"

"I get that. It took me quite a while before I was willing to play at one of Finn's parties. I only observed at the first one. The next few after that, Finn and I played beforehand and I continued to observe at the party. Of course, Finn being Finn, concessions have a price. He was lenient the first couple of times. But once I'd become more comfortable with the group generally, and playing with him in particular, the deal was, I could keep some clothes on if I played, but none if I watched. By the time I finally participated fully, I didn't need clothes to play because I was already used to being seen without them."

"But that's so mean."

"It is, and it isn't. For me it's not, because Finn has proven to me time and again that he can be trusted to know what I need and provide it using whatever method he deems necessary. In return, I have proven capable of appropriately using my safewords, yellow when I need a minute or to change something, and red to bail completely. In our house, safewords work for everything, not just kinky sex."

Hildy took a deep breath and let it out. "It's all so over-whelming."

"That's true of most things when you're first learning. I bet Sully bombarded you with tonnes of material to read, didn't he?"

"Did he ever. Of course, I've read it all, a lot of it more than once."

Mac laughed. "Of course you did, and I bet those parts you reread are the ones that got you all hot and bothered and thinking about Wilson, weren't they?"

Heat flooded Hildy's cheeks and she was thankful Mac couldn't see her. "No comment."

"That's an excellent start. I need to go run some errands, but before I leave, I'll fire off that check-list to you so you can get started on it. I'll call you later to see how you're doing. Okay?"

"That would be great. Thanks for all your help, Mac. I really appreciate you taking the time."

"It's nothing. I'm so glad you thought of me. I'd hate for you to be trying to figure this all on your own. Promise you'll call when you need someone to talk to, okay?"

"I promise. I'll let you get to your errands."

"Remember ,trust and accept yourself whilst filling out the check-list. There are no right or wrong answers to those questions for anyone but you."

"Thanks Mac, I'll talk to you soon."

"See ya."

Hildy trekked to the kitchen to make herself a cup of tea and a snack in anticipation of the mysterious check-list. What a relief she'd managed to find a woman she could talk to about this crazy stuff without fear of being judged. She had some idea of Mac's past, and she was sure Mac had knowledge of her own. They couldn't both be such close friends with Sully and not expect some aspects of their lives to bleed through. She wished she'd met Mac sooner, but it was hardly surprising she hadn't, knowing what she did about Mac's many years of isolation.

***

WIL RECOGNISED the number on the incoming call. More meddling, no doubt.

"Mac, what a surprise. To what do I owe the pleasure?"

"What are your intentions toward Hildy?"

"Excuse me?"

"You heard me."

"I answer to nobody, sub."

"You can fuck that for a lark, Wil. The only person on the planet who can boss me around is Finn, although, I do let Sully believe he has that kind of power. Seriously, Wil, what's the deal?"

"Why do you want to know?"

"I just got off the phone after having a very interesting conversation with her and I need to know how best to proceed."

"Why didn't you call Sully?"

"Because Sully is effectively her family, and one does not ask family for advice on how to advise another family member as regards the realm of all things kinky. Let's face it, there is a very real possibility of you becoming her Dom."

"When did relationship by committee get enacted?"

"Oh for fuck's sake, Wil, stop being ridiculous."

"Hang on just a minute. I've got Sully essentially telling me I have to be her Dom, and then I have you pestering me for advice on how to deal with Hildy because you figure I'm going to be her Dom. While I did agree to a trial on the physical aspects with Hildy, I only agreed to do this after Sully has her fully prepared. How you got mixed up in all this, I can't begin to understand."

"That part is easy. Sully sent Hildy a whole pile of material to read, which she did. It made her so confused and crazy, she didn't know where to turn. Fortunately for you two bozos, she called me, and I set her straight. For the moment, anyway. Now, I called you for some guidance on how best to help your new sub navigate her journey through the land of kink. Are you going to help, or do you want to take your chances on my judgement?"

"To be fair, you have excellent judgement, and I could reasonably trust you to handle this on your own. That said, you did ask for my input, so I am happy to help where I can."

"Good. Hildy is worried about being a newbie. She's freaked about not knowing what to do, how to act, and I think more importantly, that she won't like it. I asked her if she'd filled out a check-list and she hadn't. I can't imagine this was neglected on purpose, so I sent her the standard one used by Dominant Cord members."

"Dammit."

"Please don't tell me it wasn't a simple over-sight on Sully's part."

"It was rather carefully orchestrated on his part, actually."

"Then he's a buffoon, and you aren't much better for agreeing to it."

"What did you tell her?"

"We talked about trust, and how she had to trust herself first. I told her to be honest with herself and accept her answers without considering anyone else because as far as the rest of the world is, there are no right or wrong answers."

"See, this is exactly why I trust your judgement. I think you handled that perfectly. Thank you for doing this. I have a feeling our original plan could have back-fired big time. Maybe Sully and I should leave Hildy's education entirely to you."

"Oh no you don't. You're not getting off that easily. I think you will need to get involved long before there is likely to be any physical activities. I asked her if she was going to attend the play party. She declined, but I think I may be able to persuade her to come. That is, if you two dolts don't fuck it up."

"Dammit, I've never felt so useless about dealing with a woman in my life. I keep doing all the wrong things, and the thing that makes me crazy is this time I think getting it right really matters. For both of us."

"The good news is, she seems to want to get it right for both of you too. I told her to fill out the check-list and I'd call her tonight to talk about it. I would humbly suggest you fill out a shiny new check-list of your own."

"Yeah. Thanks, Mac. I'm glad Hildy has you looking out for her."

"No worries. I'll talk to you later."

"See ya." Wilson ended the call and sat for a moment to let the conversation sink in. Hildy was definitely inter-ested, but feeling self-conscious about her inexperience. Fuck. He wasn't just feeding Sully a line when he said he wasn't into playing with newbies. He liked experienced subs he could trust to know their limits. However, he was surprised to find he hated the idea of anyone else touching her, more than he feared fucking it all up for both of them. Mac said to fill out a new check-list, so he'd best get to it. He hadn't known Mac very long, but so far, she'd shown herself to be smart and wise, with a huge heart.

HILDY WASN'T GENERALLY one to procrastinate, but she had been dreading this call from the moment she'd made her decision.

"Hi Sully, how are you?"

"I'm great, Hildy. How about you? I understand you spoke with Mac."

"I'm fine and yes, Mac and I talked."

"Anything you want to ask me?"

"Nope."

"Will you be joining me at Finn and Mac's this evening?"

She forced herself to speak. "Um, yeah."

"Great, Wilson and I'll be there to pick you up at six."

"But the party doesn't start until half-seven."

"Yeah, but Wilson will have to drive slowly, and this way you can have some time with Mac before the others arrive."

"Sully?"

"What's the matter, kiddo?"

"I know it's none of my business, but..."

Hildy was grateful Sully didn't make her finish the question before answering. "No, sweetie, Wil is not bringing a playmate. That doesn't mean he won't play tonight, though."

"If he doesn't bring someone, then who would he play with?"

"Calm down, you've got a way to go before there's any chance of you playing with anyone. Sometimes Doms, particularly those who have specialised skills, will help another Dom with his sub. Wil is particularly skilled at rope bondage, and occasionally he is called upon to demonstrate a technique or even do all the rope-work so a Dom is able to concentrate on doing other things to his sub."

"Oh." That didn't answer her question, but she wasn't going to ask it a second time.

"By the way, bring your check-list with you."

"News flash, Sully, you aren't getting so much as a peek at my check-list, so I think it's just as well it stays here."

"Honey, For your own safety, someone besides your Dom will need to know exactly what's on that list. Even the most experienced Doms can make a mistake, overlook a limit, or get caught up in the moment. At times like that, even the most experienced sub could fail to safeword, but the risk is so much higher with someone who is inexperienced. You've even admitted to feeling self-conscious about your lack of knowledge and experience. It's those kinds of feelings that could stop a sub from safewording when she really should because she doesn't want to be judged as lacking. Who better than someone who has no sexual interest in you to ensure the scene goes as smoothly as possible?"

"I get it," Hildy said, "but I don't want you to know what turns me on."

"Honey, I don't want to know what turns you on,

either, but I sure as fuck want to know what turns you off. I understand, I really do. I promise only to look at the soft and hard limits. I want your experiences to be positive so you can assess your feelings fairly. Most importantly, I want you to have fun and feel great."

"Jeez. It'll be like telling my brother my innermost sexual fantasies."

"I'll try hard not to make it like that. Look on it like I'm a referee at a sporting event. My purpose is to know the rules and make sure everybody plays by them. In this case, the rules are your soft and hard limits. Okay?"

"I'm still not comfortable with this."

"I know, but I love you, and I won't trust your absolute safety in this to anyone but myself. So, either I get a copy, or you don't play."

"I could go to a club," Hildy threatened.

"Not unless you want that bottom of yours every colour of the rainbow. Going to Mac with questions is great, but I draw the line at you looking outside the safety of the quintet to explore the world of kink. Most people adhere to Safe, Sane and Consensual, but it's not a risk I'm going to let you take."

"You are such a control-freak, Sully."

"I love you, and want you to have only the good things in life. I consider the right kink with the right person, or people to be one of those good things, and I'll do what I can to make it happen for you."

"Thank you. I know, deep down, you only want my happiness. I still have a hard time accepting there are people who wish me good rather than harm."

"I know, but you'll get there. I'm going to go now, and I'll see you at six."

"Okay, have a great rest of your afternoon." Hildy waited for the click before she put her phone down. When she'd filled out that damn check-list, she hadn't expected Sully would want to see it. She wondered if she had time to change it, but even as the thought entered her head, she heard Mac telling her to be truthful with herself and there were no right or wrong answers. Besides, Sully did say he would only pay attention to the stuff that turned her off. He'd never let her down before, so she'd trust him.

Fuck. She reached for her phone and dialled. She didn't wait for Mac to say hello. "I need help."

"Oh, sweetie, what can I do?"

"I don't have a clue what to wear tonight."

"Wear whatever you feel comfortable in. You're not playing, and I can assure you, everyone will be too occupied with their own situation to pay any attention to you, or what you're wearing. I know that sounds kind of rude, and self-centred, but it's true. It's a private party, not a club, so there is no dress-code beyond a sub wearing whatever her Dom decides."

"Thanks, Mac. I appreciate you being around for me."

"Anytime, honey. You're coming early, right?"

"Yeah, Sully and Wilson are picking me up at six. Sully said being early would give you and me some time together."

"Perfect. I'll see you when you get here and we'll have a nice chat."

"Okay. See ya."

"Bye."

FOUR

Hildy smiled as Mac greeted them at the door. "Hi there. Hildy, how about you come with me whilst Sully and Wilson head down to help Finn in the dungeon." Wilson and Sully looked at each other and shrugged.

Mac took Hildy by the hand and led her to the bedroom. "I need to finish getting ready. Finn and I have some special plans tonight, and I wanted to talk to you about them."

"Why would you need to talk to me about plans you have with Finn?"

Mac sat on the bed and invited Hildy to join her. "You are very new and I want you to be prepared for the worst possible scenario. I don't know how much you know about my past, but I'll give you a quick run-down of the sordid details to help you understand the situation.

"I was bound to a piano bench and raped at the end of my first year of university." Mac paused, rubbing her palms up and down her thighs.

"As a result, I suffered from severe performance anxiety

and withdrew to the point where Sully was the only person I maintained a relationship with. Long story short, Sully's injury was the cause of Finn and me getting together and with Finn's love and patience, I've been slowly conquering my fears."

She gave Hildy a half smile. "I've got to the point where Finn can restrain me with leather cuffs, but so far, we've not tried using rope.

"Finn and I had a long talk, and we decided that we would ask Wil for help. Something very simple that is quick and easy to remove. Wilson will be completely in charge of the rope while Finn keeps me otherwise occupied.

"We've planned it to the last detail, but it could go very, very wrong, and I could totally freak out. If that happens, I need you to absolutely understand that I am in complete control of the situation. Nothing will happen that I haven't already consented to. I am pretty good about safewording for myself, but even if I don't, it is likely Finn will realise there is a problem and halt the scene before I even come close to losing it." Mac caught Hildy's gaze. "I need you to promise me you'll stay put and stay calm if things go really bad."

Hildy struggled with the discomfort she felt over Mac's decision to put her physical and emotional safety into the hands of others. "Fuck, Mac. Seriously, why would you take a chance like this?"

"Because some miserable little fucker in my past stole so much from me, and I want it back. All of it. You haven't given me your promise."

She was still uncomfortable about the situation, but she could understand Mac's motivation. "I promise."

"Thank you. I was a little conflicted about doing this at

your first party, but in the end, I decided it would be a good learning experience for you regardless of the outcome. If it all goes to shit in a handbag, you will see how loving Doms deal with a scene gone wrong. And if it all goes right, you'll see how a Dom can successfully help his sub overcome her fears."

"I don't know, Mac. Maybe I should go home. You don't need me here to complicate the situation."

"I would like you to be here. But, if it gets to be too much for you, all you have to do is say red to Sully, and he'll get you out of there. All I ask is if you do need to leave, do it quickly and quietly so you don't disturb any scenes."

"I'll try."

"Good enough. That's all anyone should ever ask of you, is to try. Now, let me get changed real quick, and we can head down to check on the fellas."

Hildy's eyes went wide as Mac rose and stripped down to a thong and corset. "Oh, before I forget, there will be sex. Lots of sex, and it's highly unlikely any of it will be soft and gentle. More importantly, you need to be prepared for women being hit. Not just with bare hands, but with all manner of paddles and hitty-sticks. I don't know if anything really prepares you for the first time you see a Dom strike his sub. It's quite shocking, and I know for me, horrifying to feel titillated by it. That's normal. The sub is in control. She has a safeword, and unless the couple have a long-standing relationship, scenes are generally carefully scripted."

"I don't know about this, Mac."

"It'll be fine. There's a first time for everything, and it's rarely as bad as we anticipate. Sully will be with you the whole time, and with the exception of our small scene, Wilson will be too. Ready?"

"As I'll ever be, I suppose."

HILDY LAUGHED when she saw Sully languishing on the fainting couch. "Oh my god. Seriously? You are an even bigger diva than I thought."

"Not this time. This was Finn's idea all the way. I gave in gracefully."

Mac nearly choked on the water she was drinking. "More like went down kicking and screaming, as I recall."

Hildy giggled. "That sounds a little more like Sully."

"I knew it would be a huge mistake for you two to ever meet."

Mac glared at Sully. "I'm pissed at you for not doing it sooner."

"Me too. Bad Sully."

"Finn, are you going to let your sub treat me like this?"

"Hell yeah. Better you than me, my friend."

Mac shot a look at Finn and he turned to Hildy. "Can you give me a hand bringing stuff down from the kitchen, Hildy?"

"Sure, lead the way."

As SOON AS they were out of earshot, Wilson watched Mac turn on Sully, wagging her finger in his face. "You pay close attention to Hildy, particularly during my scene with

Finn and Wil. I've told her the details and what could be the worst case scenario. I told her to use red if she needs you to get her out of here. I know you feel responsible for both of us, but in this instance, I need your first priority to be Hildy. I will have both Finn and Wil to take care of me."

"I don't want you to worry, love, I'll take good care of her."

"Thanks, Sully."

"Mac, are you sure you want to go through with this? I'm concerned about you pushing yourself too far, too fast."

"I'm sure Sully. Finn and I had another long talk about it this morning."

Wilson was surprised when Sully's attention was turned on him. "You'd best keep the right head in the right game. I don't want you concerning yourself over how Hildy's doing when you're working on Mac. Clear?"

"Normally, I'd be offended, but considering how my interest in Hildy has already impaired my judgement once, I'll take the warning in the spirit in which it was meant. However, whilst I am working on Mac, I'm trusting you to focus all your attention on Hildy's well-being for me."

"Now you've both flexed your penises, can we move on to more interesting subjects?" Mac asked.

***

HILDY SAT NEXT TO SULLY, fascinated by the activities going on around her, but her attention kept wandering back to Wilson.

"How are you doing, sweetie?"

"Oh, I'm fine. Stop fussing like a maiden aunt." The words had barely spilled from her lips before the first blow of the evening fell on naked flesh and was followed by a long, low moan. She swung her head in the direction of the sounds and her jaw dropped at the sight. There sat Finn with Mac draped over his lap and his hand poised to strike again. She was appalled at her reaction. Part of her was sure she was witnessing abuse and she should step in to put a stop to it, but the larger part of her was aroused and even envious. Mac's words echoed in her head about the sub being in charge. Still, she'd best check with Sully. He'd never sit by and let something bad happen.

As she turned, ready to ask her question, Sully smiled and said, "She's just fine. Finn is going to get her flying a bit before he brings Wilson in with the rope."

"If you're sure."

"I am positive. If Finn and Mac's scene makes you uncomfortable, I can set you up somewhere else to observe other activities, or take you upstairs."

"No, I think I'll be okay. I was just a little surprised."

"You handled it well. If you are going to continue watching this scene, I really need you to keep your head. Mac has safewords and two experienced Doms watching her closely for any signs of a problem. Finn is madly in love with her and would slice off both his hands with a rusty band-saw before risking her physical or emotional safety. No matter what you think is happening, you absolutely must stay quiet and out of the way."

Hildy nodded. "I know. Mac went over it with me earlier."

"In that case, settle yourself down, I think the show is about to really begin."

Hildy returned her attention to Mac and Finn's scene. She wasn't prepared for the snarl of jealousy and want she felt when Wilson stepped into the scene area, shirtless and ripped. She squirmed subconsciously in her seat as she scrutinised every naked inch of his torso.

Finn had shifted Mac so she was sitting on his lap, her back against his chest and her legs spread outside of his own. He peppered the crook of her neck with tiny kisses as he took hold of one nipple and pulled it away from her body. He attached a clover clamp on it and let it drop. She'd barely let out a moan before he'd done the same to her other nipple.

Finn lifted his lips to Mac's ear. "Colour, love?"

"I'm green."

The exchange was barely audible, but it helped reduce Hildy's concern. She stole a look at Wilson. He was focused on Finn and Mac, apparently oblivious to everything else going on around him. Finn gave a barely perceptible nod, and as Wilson moved toward the couple, she knew this was as it should be, but she still struggled with the twinges of jealousy that kept pinching her heart.

She flinched, then relaxed when she realised the hand touching her arm belonged to Sully. "He's doing a favour. Nothing more. You don't have to stay."

Hildy turned her head slightly, but didn't take her eyes off the threesome. "No, I'll be fine."

"Okay, but I reserve the right to call red for you if I think it's getting too much for you." Hildy nodded.

Finn took one of Mac's hands and moved it so her arm was positioned straight out in front of her. "Don't move until I tell you otherwise."

"Okay."

"Good girl," Finn said. He gave Wilson another quick nod as he settled a vibrator over Mac's clit and flipped the switch. Mac immediately started rolling her hips. Finn pulled the vibrator away then flicked a crop across Mac's clamped nipples. "I said don't move."

Hildy inhaled sharply and Sully's hand tightened on her arm when she tried to rise from her seat. "Trust me, she's fine. She wouldn't be smiling if she wasn't. Now breathe."

Hildy nodded and took a slow, deep breath as she settled back down, focusing her attention back to Mac's scene.

Mac's head was tilted back and resting on Finn's shoulder. Her eyes were closed and there was no mistaking her expression for anything but bliss.

Wilson stood in front of Mac with a length of purple rope in his hand. He doubled it in half and wrapped it around Mac's wrist, slowly bringing the two loose ends through the folded part of the rope. Then he stopped. Mac was quivering. Finn stroked his knuckles down her cheek. "Colour, love?"

"Yellow"

"Okay. Can we leave the rope where it is, or do you need Wil to take it off?"

"I don't know."

"It's a binary question, Mac. On or off?"

Mac chewed on her lip for a minute, then said, "On. I think I'm okay to carry on."

Finn clearly had other ideas. "I think we'll take a minute or two before we continue." Wilson stepped back and Finn reached back to the little table set to his right and a little behind and grabbed a small tube along with what Hildy now knew to be a butt-plug.

Hildy's hand flew to her mouth, but she watched in morbid fascination as Mac's ass swallowed the plug Finn had generously slathered with lube. She flicked a quick glance in Wilson's direction, noting the detachment with which he watched, before returning her attention to the scene.

Finn repositioned Mac and signalled Wilson to come back. Wilson approached, stopping next to Finn. He leaned down and said something too softly for Hildy to catch. Finn nodded, and Wilson crouched in front of Mac. "I need to hear you tell me you want to continue."

"I'm green."

"No, tell me exactly what you want me to do. I need to hear you say the words, Mac. I will not do this without them."

"I want you to use rope on me exactly like we discussed."

"What did we agree on, Mac?"

"Nothing more than simple arm gauntlets."

"Very good. Are you ready?"

"Yes."

Wilson took hold of the abandoned rope dangling from Mac's wrist and tied a series of loops and knots around her forearm, stopping to check in after each. Mac's breathing seemed rather erratic, but considering the careful attention both Doms were paying to her every move and sound, along with the distractions Finn was providing, Hildy suspected Mac was more likely ready to orgasm than panic.

With the first gauntlet finished Finn removed the

vibrator from Mac's clit and gently guided her arm down to her side.

"Ready for the next one, love?"

"I'd rather come."

"Soon, baby. One more gauntlet, then you can come, okay?"

"But I want to come now, you've had me on edge forever. Why can't I have an orgasm now and another after the next gauntlet, dammit?"

"Mac," Finn warned.

"Fuck, I hate this. I just want to come."

"Are you safewording?"

"Will it get me an orgasm faster?"

"Do not try to manipulate me, Mac Wallis. You know it won't end well."

"But Finn..."

"Enough."

Mac pursed her lips together, and dropped her head backwards onto Finn's shoulder.

Hildy was shocked by the exchange. She turned towards Sully and whispered, "I don't understand. I thought subs were supposed to be quiet unless they safeword or are given permission to speak."

"As long as it's Safe, Sane, Consensual, and works for all parties involved, it's all good. Sometimes Doms and subs find dynamic preferences change with the company they keep. Finn used to be one of those strict Doms who punished bratty behaviour hard and fast. Then he met Mac. She has to be pretty outrageous before he'll give her a real punishment for it, and he's particularly tolerant when they're doing a scene and she's pushing her limits. As you can see, she is learning when to stop. Are you still okay?"

"Yeah, I think so. It's all so confusing. I see stuff that gets me kind of excited, but I feel guilty."

"Yeah, it can take some getting used to, but the only way for that to happen is to keep exposing yourself to it in a safe and controlled manner."

"I know I threatened to explore this through other avenues, but I'm glad you put your foot down. I don't think I could have handled this around strangers."

Sully patted her hand and motioned back to the scene.

Finn had returned the vibrator to Mac's clit, and Wilson was just tying off the second gauntlet. As soon as Wilson removed his hands, Finn adjusted something on the vibrator and whispered in Mac's ear. Her hips and legs started to shake, and as she began to wail, Wilson stepped in and removed the clamps from Mac's nipples before slipping away.

Mac's wails subsided and Finn spoke. "You've been such a good, brave girl, Mac. One more, then I have some nice chocolate for you."

Mac barely acknowledged Finn's words before it was obvious to all she'd been consumed by another orgasm. As soon as Finn discarded the vibrator, Wilson returned and handed him a nice soft looking blanket that was different from the others scattered about the dungeon. Hildy mentally smacked herself, of course, Mac would have her own personal blanket, she lived here.

Finn carefully wrapped the blanket around Mac and carried her to the after-care area, where he sat on a sofa and settled her in his lap. When Hildy saw the content look on Mac's face, she felt a little lonely and a lot envious.

Men were for sexual release and nothing more. Use them before they use you. Now, for the first time she could recall, she felt like she wanted a connection that went deeper than the length of a man's cock.

She was jolted from her thoughts when she felt a pair of arms wrap a soft blanket around her. She started to lean in, then she realised those arms didn't belong to Sully. She snapped her head around to see Wilson wearing a sheepish grin. "What do you think you are doing?"

"After-care, love."

Hildy slipped the blanket off and opened her mouth to speak, but Sully interrupted. "Hildy, we agreed that Wilson would be the one to provide you with practical experience. At least temporarily, that makes Wilson your Dom, and you his sub. Now, consider the situation from his point of view. His sub has just pushed her boundaries well outside her comfort zone. As a Dom, he can't, in good conscience, leave you to deal with it alone. So, here he is trying to take care of your needs and ensure your first experiences as a sub are as positive as possible."

"It's all so damn complicated."

"It usually is, if it's worth having. Now, can I leave you with Wilson and trust you'll let him do whatever he deems necessary to care for you?"

"I don't know."

Wilson interjected. "Safewords work for everything, Hildy. Yellow to pause or make a change, and red if you really can't handle it. Can you give me a chance?"

Hildy turned to Sully for help. One look at his cold eyes, and she wasn't surprised by his parting words. "Safeword and we'll go. Otherwise, Wilson is in charge." Hildy dropped her head in defeat.

"Hildy?" Wilson's voice was soft and patient as he tipped her chin up with his index finger. "Look at me, please."

Hildy couldn't bear to see the pity she knew his eyes would hold, so she kept her own focused on the floor.

"Hildy, please, I want to talk with you, but eye to eye, as equals, not Dom and sub. Not yet."

Hildy was so absorbed in her study of the dungeon floor, she was unprepared for Wilson's smiling face to block her view.

"There you are. If this is how you want to talk, I can go with it."

Hildy shifted her gaze to the side, and Wilson followed. Frustrated, she looked straight into his eyes. "I don't want to talk right now."

"Fair enough, then safeword out and Sully will take you home."

"No, I'm not a wimp."

"Hold it right there. Wimp? Did you think Mac was being a wimp when she called yellow?"

"No, of course not. That's different."

"No, Hildy, it's not. Nobody is ever a wimp for using a safeword. Are there times when someone abuses it? Of course. In the end, it's their loss, but that still doesn't make them a wimp. Understand?"

"Yes."

"Good girl. Now, can we have this conversation in a more comfortable position? Don't get me wrong, I am willing to have it however you need it to be, but I'm not a fan of crouching for long periods of time."

"Yet you lot expect your subs to always be on their knees."

"We'll get to that misconception in a minute. Can you please answer me? More comfortable position?"

"Okay."

"Thank you." Wilson stood and snagged a nearby chair. He set it down facing Hildy and sat. "Now, as for subs on their knees all the time. Some Doms? Sure. Me? No."

"Why not?"

"It's not my thing. Now isn't the time to go into detail about what is and isn't my thing or your thing. If you've brought your check-list with you, we'll exchange them when we leave and go over them at our leisure. Okay?"

"Okay."

"Good. Next. You've denied me one of my favourite parts of being a Dom, and I would like to fix that now."

"What do you want to do?"

"Give you the after-care you need."

Hildy glanced over at Mac, still snuggled up on Finn's lap and surrendered to that stab of envy she'd felt earlier.

"Okay."

"Good girl. I know that was hard for you. I want to wrap you back up in that blanket and carry you over to where Finn and Mac are, where I am going to snuggle you in my lap and feed you chocolate. Tell me you like chocolate."

"I love chocolate."

Wilson rose from his chair and gathered the blanket back around Hildy. He swooped her into his arms and held her close. She closed her eyes and let her head relax against his chest as she tried to make sense of the jittery feeling she had deep in her belly.

HILDY PANICKED until Wilson's soft voice washed over her.

"You're okay, love. You just had a little nap is all."

"What's going on?" Hildy panicked again and as she struggled, her bonds loosened.

"Hildy, calm down. You fell asleep."

Hildy's mind raced back through the events of the evening before she came up with the only explanation she could for falling asleep as she did. "Did you drug me?"

Mac gasped and Finn's head whirled round to glare at Hildy. She stiffened. "Well, did you?"

Wilson inhaled long and deep. "I can understand why you might think that, love, especially when you're still a bit groggy from an unexpected nap, but take a few minutes. Think about Sully — who, and what he is to you. Then think about whether he would ever put you, or anyone for that matter, in a situation where that could possibly happen. I'll still be here, waiting, when you have your answer."

Hildy pulled the blanket over her head and tighter around her body as she curled into a ball.

"You're going to have to come out sometime, love. I'll be here when you do."

The last thing Hildy expected after she exhibited such abominable behaviour, was to feel Wilson pull her tight to him and stroke his hand up and down her back. She squirmed in discomfort. It was getting hot and stuffy under the blanket. She wanted to come out, but she didn't want Wilson to stop what he was doing, and worse, she didn't want to see the people who must be staring at her making such a spectacle of herself.

"Hildy, are you ready to come out?"

"No."

"Nobody's paying any attention to you. Jack's got Sloane bent over the spanking bench and is laying into her ass with the seat strap from his bassoon and Griff is keeping her mouth busy. Sub in a blanket just can't compete with that."

Hildy shifted the blanket enough to see from one eye. Sure enough, Wilson was telling the truth, not one person in the room was looking at her. Except him. She moved the blanket to expose more of her head. The air in the room felt chilly on her sweaty head and caused her whole body to shiver. She looked up into Wilson's face, and his stony expression contradicted his gentle strokes up and down her back.

"Do you have an answer for me?"

"No, Sully would never, ever do that."

"You're damn right he wouldn't. In addition, by accusing me of drugging you, you are accusing everyone in this room of being complicit. You've essentially branded every person here as untrustworthy. You owe them all an apology, Hildy, but I don't think sorry is going to cut it.

"I'm going to have to decide on an appropriate apology, and once I do, you will have two options. Either you apologise exactly as I tell you, or you safeword out and you won't be welcome to play here.

"Fair warning, I won't make this easy on you. Trust is what everything balances on here. I thought you understood that. Questioning someone's integrity, especially in public, without good reason is beyond serious. If you aren't able to treat those around you, especially Sully, with the same respect they've afforded you, then you need to safe-word out now."

Hildy couldn't hold back the tears any longer. Her parents were right, she was stupid. She should have stayed home.

WILSON WAS TORN. He knew damn well her accusation wasn't meant. She fell asleep so fast after that chocolate, it was hardly surprising she would think she'd been drugged. However, deep down she knew Sully would never put her at risk like that, and had she controlled her tongue until her brain was fully engaged, she wouldn't be in this fix. He wished he could tell her it was just a mistake and every-thing is fine. Unfortunately, he couldn't. As a Dom, he could never let his sub get away with something like this. If she wanted to continue to explore her kinky side, she abso-lutely had to make amends. Word would get around. Jackson and Griff rarely had a regular sub although, if he wasn't mistaken, this one broke the record for most appear-ances. It was made clear to subs who came to play at Finn's parties, that they were private and what happened at Finn's stayed at Finn's. But everyone also understood it was an unrealistic expectation, and they governed their behaviour accordingly. He had a fairly good idea of what would be a fitting punishment for Hildy, but he needed to ensure the rest of the group understood just how much she would struggle with it.

"Hildy, I need to go have a quick chat with Sully. Will you be okay on your own for a minute?"

He knew she was still crying, so accepted her nod

rather than a proper answer. This time. He gently shifted her sideways, off his lap and onto the sofa. "I'll be back as soon as I can and we'll get this sorted." He didn't expect an answer, so he didn't wait.

He headed straight for Sully, who was parked in front of Jack's scene. He positioned himself to Sully's side and whispered, "I need to talk to you. It's urgent."

"Sully's head swivelled towards Wilson as he glared. "What. Did. You. Do?"

"Hush, just come with me now. We need to hurry."

Sully got up and followed Wilson to a quiet corner of the room. "I didn't do anything." Wilson filled Sully in on what happened and what he planned to do about it. "So, I need you to discretely give the heads-up. You and I both know this is going to be really hard for Hildy to do, and I need to be sure everyone else understands. Particularly Sloane. She's the one most likely to blow this into a complete clusterfuck."

"I'll get Mac to help me. You get back to Hildy. Understand though, for Hildy's sake, beyond getting the word out, I have to stay completely out of this."

"I know, and I respect that."

Sully gave Wilson a quick pat on the shoulder before embarking on his mission. Wilson spun on his heel and returned to the sofa. "Okay, love. Here's the deal. The best way to apologise and prove you didn't mean what you implied is to give them a demonstration of your trust."

"How am I supposed to do that?"

"By doing something you're going to find really hard. With the exception of Sully and myself, you are going to say you're sorry to each person here and give them a hug, which has to last at least ten seconds after they've wrapped their arms around you."

Hildy buried her face in her hands. "There is no way I can do that. How could you possibly ask that of me?"

Wilson wanted to take her in his arms and sooth her, but that would have to wait until either she apologised to the others or safeworded out. "If it's easy for you, it will mean nothing to them. It's easy to say you're sorry. It's a lot harder to prove it. Mending broken trust is harder still. You broke their trust in you, Hildy. You have to earn it back, and the best way to do that is trust them with something you find hard. If this really is too much for you, then safe-word out and I'll take you home."

"I guess your trust is broken too?"

"Nothing that can't be fixed if you want it to."

"I don't know, Wil. You know how I am about being touched."

"Exactly. It's something we were going to work on at some point, but, I sure as hell wasn't expecting it to be at your first play party."

"I'm so, so sorry, Wil."

"Enough. You need to have a hard think about what you're going to do because you don't have much time to make your decision. Jack and Griff look to be close to finishing their scene."

Wilson waited patiently as he watched Hildy struggle with her decision. That she didn't immediately bail confirmed his initial impression. She didn't give up easily. Based on what little he knew of her horrendous childhood, she could very easily have stopped fighting.

"I'll try."

Wilson smiled and reached for her hand to help her up

from the sofa. "Try is good. We'll go by sub then her Dom, starting with Mac. By the time we've gone through everyone, Jack, Griff, and Sloane should be just about ready for you."

"Wilson?"

"Yes, love?"

"What do I have to do to apologise to you and Sully?"

"We'll get to that later. As far as Griff, Jack, and Sloane are concerned, your apology to us is a private matter to be witnessed by Mac and Finn."

"I don't understand."

"All they need to know is you'll be making appropriate apologies to all involved. They will see you making enough of your apologies in public to be assured you will follow through with the private ones."

"I'm sorry I ruined your night."

"Enough. It's time to go find Mac and Finn."

***

WHAT HAVE I DONE? Hildy worked hard to keep her breathing slow and regular. Her heart was pounding and her palms were sweaty as Wilson led her to make her first apology. Mac. This she could do. She knew Mac. She'd been nothing but kind and supportive, and this was the least she could do after fucking up so badly. She looked to Finn as she approached Mac. He gave a nod, and she stepped forward. "I'm so sorry, Mac. I didn't mean to abuse your trust."

Mac pulled her into her embrace. "No harm done, You're forgiven." Then she whispered into Hildy's ear, "Call me later, we'll talk."

After what seemed like forever, Wilson spoke. "Alright, break it up you two."

Once Mac finally let her go, Hildy turned to Finn and repeated her apology. She thought she was going to pass out when he took her into his arms and gave her a firm, but gentle hug. "Brave girl, you make us proud. You're forgiven, pet."

With each apology, the hugs became less difficult. She felt her chest get lighter as she realised she was down to Griff, Jack, and their sub. She was almost done and nothing bad happened.

She approached Sloane and made her apologies. Unlike the rest of the group who were gracious and welcoming, she waited for Hildy to make body contact and even then, she didn't wrap her arms around Hildy until Jack reminded her. She brought her lips close to Hildy's ear and whispered, "You'll never be forgiven, loser." before pulling away with a glib, "Forgiven."

Hildy was crushed and her face fell. She just wanted to run away, and she was so close to doing just that. Then she caught sight of Sully, nodding his head in silent encouragement. Sully. Two more apologies. Two more hugs. She could do it. Make Sully proud, then she could leave with her head held high and never see these people again.

She lifted her head and turned to apologise to Jack. This time, she couldn't quite meet his eyes. She tried to make this apology sound as sincere as the rest, but her heart wasn't in it. She struggled to get the words out, before creeping her way into Jack's arms for the mandatory hug. It took an eternity and it was all she could do not to tear herself from his arms and flee. Instead, she stiffened her spine and turned to deliver her final apology.

"That's it, she's done." Hildy never thought she would be so glad to hear Wilson's voice. She forced herself to disentangle from Griff's embrace with as much dignity as she could muster before seeking out the closest person she could trust in this room of liars.

It was Wilson who gathered her in his arms and carried her back to the sofa. Once she was settled back on his lap, he kissed her temple and asked, "What just happened?"

She shook her head. "Nothing, I'm fine."

"Don't ever lie to me, Hildy. What's wrong?"

Just then, a very angry Sully arrived and parked himself next to the couple. "What the fuck just happened?"

"That's what I want to know. Start talking, Hildy."

"I don't want to talk about it. I just want to go home."

"Is that a red?" Wilson asked.

Hildy was done.

"Yes, it's a fucking red, okay. Red. I'm going home." Wil released her instantly and she scrambled from his lap.

"Okay, give us a few minutes to get organised and we'll take you home."

"No, I'll call a taxi. I don't want to see any of you again. I'm done."

Hildy raced across the dungeon and up the stairs, not caring who saw or what they thought.

WILSON STARTED TO RISE, intending to go after Hildy, when he felt Sully's hand on his leg "Wil, let her go. She needs her space. She may calm down quickly and let us take her home, but she's most likely going to follow through on the cab. Regardless, you need to let her be. For now."

"Did I push her too far? She was doing so well right up until she got to Sloane."

"No, something happened between Sloane and Hildy. Go get Finn and Mac, and while you're at it, tell Jack and Griff to hang on for a few minutes."

Wilson decided to swing by Jack and Griff first before fetching Mac and Finn. He was surprised to see their sub on her knees and tears streaming down her face. He missed what Jack had to say, but he did see Sloane shaking her head emphatically. Griff looked over as Wil approached and cocked an eyebrow. A silent question.

"Can you two wait a few minutes before going? Sully and I want to have a quick word. We just need to speak with Finn and Mac first."

"Sure, no problem. In the meantime, I'll get our stuff together."

"Thanks." On his way to get Finn and Mac, Wilson briefly wondered if Jack and Griff had picked up on the sudden change in Hildy after her apology to his sub. He hoped so. It would make sorting this out much easier.

"Finn, Mac, Sully and I would like a word."

Mac shook her head. "I was just going to check on Hildy. She flew out of here like her ass was on fire."

"Sully said it's best to give her some space."

"Sully isn't always the sharpest cookie in the shed, now, is he?"

"Please, Mac? This concerns Hildy."

"Fine, but she'd better still be upstairs by the time we're done or you're in it deep, bucko."

And with that, there was no question Mac had switched from sub to protective mama-bear.

Sully started talking the moment the other three took their seats. "I assume we all saw the same thing. Hildy was doing great until she got to that sub Jack and Griff brought?" The group nodded and he carried on. "Mac, what do you think?"

"It's pretty simple, that bitch had to have said something mean to our Hildy. I was behind her and didn't actually see or hear her say anything, but I did see Hildy's face transform from nervous to devastated in the space of a second."

"Finn?"

I didn't see or hear anything either, but there was a definite and immediate change in Hildy's demeanour." Finn turned to Wilson. "What did she say?"

"Red."

"Wilson asked Jack and Griff to hang back for a few minutes. I think we should call them over now, but that sub should stay put until we've talked this through."

The group agreed, and Sully caught Jack's attention and motioned for him to join them. He spoke before anyone else had a chance. "I can only assume this little pow-wow has something to do with what happened between Hildy and Sloane?"

Wilson's eyes blazed. "What did happen?"

"Damned if I know. I asked Sloane, and she said she had no idea what the problem could be. She'd accepted Hildy's apology and that was that."

"Do you believe her?" Finn asked.

"No, I don't. I was just about to get into that with her. What did Hildy say about it?"

"First she denied there was an issue, then she refused to talk about it and called red."

"Fuck! We were really hoping things would work out with this one. I'll deal with her. Then she's done. Is Hildy still here?"

Mac jumped up from her seat. "I'll go check. If she is, what should I do?"

Wilson spoke up. "Keep her here. Do whatever you need to keep her from leaving. I know she called red over whatever went on with Sloane, but I want to make sure everything is okay between us and make sure she gets home safely."

Mac nodded and headed for the stairs.

"What do you have in mind, Jack?"

"I think Sloane needs to learn about telling the truth, and once she's confessed, I think she'll be begging Hildy for forgiveness."

"Absolutely not," Wilson objected.

"What? Why not?"

"She's fragile, Jack. Really, really fragile. If I could have found a way to keep her from having to apologise to everyone, I would have done it in a heartbeat. I wanted to say fuck it and brush it all under the rug anyway. I think the best thing we can do for her right now is keep Sloane well away from her. I'm not saying don't get the truth and mete out punishment. I'm just saying keep Hildy out if it. And Jack?" He shot the other man a pointed look. "I want Hildy kept right out of it."

"Got it. I'll get Sloane to admit the truth, then punish her for the lying. That work for you?"

"Good enough."

"Alright." Jack turned to Sully. "Could you please come and bear witness?"

"My pleasure."

Wilson felt a bit torn. Part of him wanted to watch Jack and Griff deal with their sub on Hildy's behalf, but a larger part of him wanted to be with Hildy and get things back on track. His need to be with Hildy won and he quietly made his way out of the dungeon, sparing only a passing glance and a twinge of pity for the sub who'd earned punishment at Jack's hand. He'd call Sully later for the details.

His heart broke when he walked into the living room to see Hildy sobbing in Mac's arms. He caught Mac's eye and put a finger to his lips as he made his way towards the sofa. Once he'd crouched in front of Hildy, he gave Mac a quick nod.

"Hildy, Wilson is here, and he wants to talk to you."

As Hildy lifted her head, Wilson took her hand in his and gently rubbed his thumb along her fingers.

"Hildy?"

She slowly met his gaze, but didn't speak.

"Aw, honey, I'm so sorry. Can I please hold you?"

Hildy remained silent, but nodded.

Mac eased away so Wilson could take her place.

"Oh, sweet Hildy, I'm sorry I pushed. I know you don't want to talk about it, so you don't have to. I'm just going to tell you what we know and what's going on. Okay?"

Hildy nodded again, and Wilson continued. "We know Sloane said something to upset you. We all knew it the moment it happened. None of us know what she said, but it was obvious to all, it wasn't even remotely charitable. Jack noticed too, honey. He asked her. She lied to him, and he knew it. After chatting with us, he decided to get the truth out of her and then he'll punish her for lying. While I would like her to get all the punishment she deserves for her actions, Jack is making sure you are in no way connected to why she is being punished. She's not welcome here, and there is no reason why you should ever encounter her again. Okay?"

Hildy shook her head violently and croaked, "No."

"What's the problem, love?"

"I don't want to be the reason for anyone's punishment."

"You aren't. She was asked a question and she lied. We've talked about trust. You had a punishment of your own for breaking it. Lying is not tolerated and is always, always severely punished. It's not your fault."

"Yes it is. If I hadn't screwed up, she wouldn't have lied."

"Maybe not tonight, but I can assure you, she would at some point. She was willing to lie thinking it would keep her out of trouble. That kind of thinking doesn't have a sell-by date, love. She got herself into trouble tonight, just like you did. The difference is you took responsibility for your actions and accepted the consequences. We are all very, very proud of you."

"But I screwed up."

"Yes, you did. You also accepted your punishment gracefully and have been forgiven. The slate is clean."

"Until it gets thrown in my face, you mean."

"Mac, can you please explain?"

Mac returned to the sofa and settled on the floor in front of Hildy. "He's telling you the truth, Hildy. A good

Dom doesn't bring up past transgressions once they've been punished and forgiven. Neither does a good sub."

"This is all so crazy making."

Mac patted Hildy's leg as she rose. "Stay there and rest with Wilson. You don't have to figure it all out tonight. Just know you're safe and with people who care."

Wilson rested his cheek on top of Hildy's head and quietly hummed bits of the adagio from Beethoven's *Sonata Pathetique* as he stroked his fingers up and down her arm. When her breathing evened out, he relaxed a bit and set about figuring out how to make this work, and more puzzling, why he wanted to.

HILDY STRUGGLED to stay asleep despite the tickle on her cheek and being told it was time to wake up. She finally gave in and opened her eyes to glare at the fool who dared interrupt the most peaceful sleep she'd had in recent memory. She didn't even try to hide her irritation. "What?"

"It's time to go, love. Sully is spending the night here, and while Finn and Mac have made it clear they have plenty of space and we are both welcome, I thought you'd prefer to sleep in your own bed."

Hildy shook off the sleep induced fog clouding her brain. "Yeah, I would."

"I'll get our stuff together while you get your coat and boots on, okay?"

Hildy nodded and rose from Wilson's lap, surprised at the sudden loneliness she felt. She stole a glance at him as he got to his feet, and the heat she saw in his expression shot straight to her pussy. Her boobs ached for his touch and she recklessly considered taking him home to fuck. She didn't doubt he'd be great in the sack, but she wasn't too sure about this whole kinky thing, and she couldn't imagine he did vanilla. Even if they could find sexual compatibility, the comfort and safety she felt when in his embrace was disconcerting and would make it virtually impossible to maintain a strictly fuck-buddy relationship.

She found her way to the door and pulled on her boots, preferring to wait until they were on their way out before donning her coat. It wasn't long before Wilson returned with Finn and Mac. "Sully's already headed to bed, but he sends his love," Mac said.

"Thanks Mac. Can you tell him I'll pick him up on my way to work and drop him home?"

"No, we'll get him home tomorrow. Don't you worry about a thing. Would you like me to get him to call you?"

"Maybe just tell him I'll give him a shout after work?"

"Sure thing." Mac moved in and gathered Hildy in her arms. "You call me, day or night if you need anything, or just want to talk. Okay?" Hildy nodded and Mac continued. "Fair enough. You did so well, tonight. We're all really proud of you."

Hildy nodded again, knowing her voice would betray her emotions. Mac loosened her grip and passed her into Finn's arms. "Sweet dreams, pet. We'll see you soon."

By the time Finn let Hildy go, Wilson was ready and waiting to help her into her coat. "Come on, sleepy-head. The sooner we go, the sooner you can be snoring on your own pillow."

She shot him a murderous glare. "I don't snore." The

twinkle in his eye should have irritated her more, but instead, it fed the nagging ache she felt in her heart.

Hildy waved to Mac and Finn as Wilson slipped his arm through hers and guided her through the front door. "Careful, love. The steps look a bit slippery."

It was on the tip of her tongue to be ornery, but she was tired, and he was right. "I will."

"Good girl."

"The party's over, I think you can quit with the Dom-speak now."

"Hildy, as far as I'm concerned, until I get you safely home, I'm responsible and the dynamic remains in effect."

"And if I safeword out?"

Wilson didn't respond until both he and Hildy were settled in the car. "Then we can drop the dynamic, but I have to ask you to consider carefully whether safewording in this situation would be from feeling overwhelmed and unable to deal, or just a quick and easy out?"

"It was just a question."

"And that was the answer. Are you safewording?"

"Of course not."

"Then the dynamic stays in place until I get you home."

Hildy folded her arms on her chest and snapped, "Fine."

"I can't imagine you are looking for more consequences when we haven't finished with what you've already earned tonight."

"What do you mean?"

"If you recall, you still have to apologise to Sully and me."

"I kind of hoped I was going to get let off the hook."

"Not a chance. Unless you safeword out, we'll be returning to Mac and Finn's tomorrow night to put this unpleasantness behind us."

Hildy sunk lower in her seat and sulked. She was horny, and with this punishment hanging over her head, nailing Wilson was out of the question.

"What are you thinking so hard about, love?"

"Me being stupid."

"You are not stupid."

"Yeah, I am."

"No, love, you aren't. And whenever you say it, I'll make be sure your ass will remind you every time you sit for many days to follow."

"You wouldn't."

"I know Sully doesn't let you get away with talking down about yourself like this, and you can bet that luscious ass of yours, I won't either."

The nearer they drew to Hildy's, the closer they were to separating, and the lonelier she felt. Casual sex was one of the few human interactions she was comfortable initiating. She was rarely rejected, and she had a pretty good instinct for choosing men who stayed just long enough to be polite, but never until morning. Wilson did not fit in that category. If she invited him in for a fuck, she had no doubt he would still be there when her alarm went off.

"When we get to my place, do you want to come in and fuck?" Not what she'd meant to say. Not even close.

"I have to say, love, that's probably the very last thing I expected to hear you say tonight."

"Can we pretend that didn't happen?"

"No, we can't. I do want to come in, and I do want to fuck, but only one of those things is going to happen tonight. You may want to use the time you have left before we arrive to get your head on straight. We've got some talking to do."

Hildy pressed her lips together and squeezed her eyes shut as she silently berated herself for continually being so fucking stupid.

"Saying it in your head is no different to saying it out loud, love. You are not stupid. A little impulsive, perhaps, but not stupid. You've been warned."

Hildy worked at keeping her mind blank for the remainder of the ride home. She was almost calm by the time Wil pulled his key from the ignition.

FIVE

WILSON SAT at the kitchen table in silence and watched Hildy fidgeting in the seat opposite as he considered the situation. He was in way over his head, and he had no idea what to do about it. What on earth possessed her to proposition him like that? Did she have any idea how fast her words made his cock stand up and take notice? Every single cock-deflation method he tried failed miserably. A swollen, angry penis was the worst possible distraction.

"Here's the deal, Hildy. We're both tired, so I would like to table most of the issues until morning. However, there are some that require immediate attention. Firstly, we need to talk about your proposition in the car."

"Please, Wil, can't we just forget it? I made a mistake. I'm tired and I wasn't thinking."

"That's exactly why we need to talk about this. Why are you so tired?"

"Maybe because I don't sleep very well. It takes me a long time to get to sleep, and even once I get there, I wake up a lot. I don't do medication and I've been like this my whole life, so I'm used to it."

"What about when you sleep with someone? Do you sleep better or worse?"

"The few times anyone has stayed the night meant no sleep at all, so now, I only go to bed with men who fuck and go."

"I see. Are you willing to try an experiment?"

"What kind of experiment?"

"You and I go to bed. We don't fuck, and I stay the night."

"Are you nuts? The only reason for me to let a man in my bed is so I can get my rocks off. Your proposal is the worst of both worlds."

"I'd be lying if I let you think I didn't want you with every inch of my cock. I want to ram it into your pussy over and over until we both explode. I want you on all fours while I bury it in your ass, and I really want you on your knees while you take it deep in your mouth.

"But that's not all I want. I want to work your pussy over with my mouth until you scream. I want to lick, suck, and bite your nipples until you squirm and beg me to let you come, and damn it, I want to kiss you all night long.

"I want to do all those things and more, but I won't. I won't because what you think you want, and what you need are not always the same. Tonight, you won't get what you want, but you will get what you need."

"You walk in here, get me all hot and bothered, then tell me you aren't going to do anything about it because it's not what I need?"

"Pretty much. To be fair, you are not the only one who is all hot and bothered, but you do appear to be the only one who has consistently poor impulse control. I would like to point out, the other reason I won't is because we have not had the all-important check-list talk, which I will not have whilst sporting a raging hard-on. No talk, definitely no sex.

"Fucking men who leave isn't really working for you, is it? From what you've said, it doesn't sound like it improves your sleep quality any. What's the worst that can happen if I stay the night without sexual contact?"

"I could die."

"Now you're being silly. I'll make you a deal. If you don't sleep better, we can have the check-list talk over breakfast, and I'll come back tomorrow night, fuck you six ways from Sunday, wait the appropriate amount of time, and leave. However, if you do sleep better, we have the check-list talk in the morning and then tomorrow night, I get to do anything I want within the limits of your check-list."

"Anything?"

"Anything. Unless you safeword. Deal?"

"It doesn't matter, because I know you'll lose."

"We'll see. It's getting late, so we may as well get this experiment started."

HILDY COULDN'T BELIEVE what she'd agreed to. Wilson sleep in her bed? All night, without even an orgasm? How fucking stupid was she? She finished rinsing her toothbrush and popped it in the holder on the side of the vanity.

Wilson spat out the toothpaste in his mouth and caught

her eye in the mirror. "Hildy? Don't think it. Your ass won't appreciate it, I promise you."

"How do you always know?"

"As tempting as it is to tell you it's a Dom thing, I won't. Your face doesn't hide much, love. There's this look you get when that thought pops into your head."

"Damn it. I guess I need to work on that."

"By work on that, you had better mean work on not having that thought. Because working on hiding it is no different from lying as far as I'm concerned, and the punishment for lying is probably the most severe I am ever likely to give you. Do you want to risk it?"

Hildy shook her head, but she couldn't ignore how the prospect of severe punishment made her pussy throb and leak.

"Interesting."

"What?"

"Like I said, love. Your face is like a jumbotron transmitting your thoughts to your audience. Don't worry, Hildy. It's a good thing. Come on, let's get to bed."

Hildy led the way to her bedroom and slid beneath the quilt. She lay there, trying not to let her panic show.

"Hildy, love? What is it?" She shook her head. "Please stop trying to hide it, and tell me what the problem is."

She assumed the fetal position and wrapped her arms tightly around herself, too ashamed and embarrassed to answer.

"Come on, love. No judgement. I can't help if you don't tell me how." Wilson gathered her into his arms and held her tight to his body. She was surprised at how much better this felt than being the filling in a quilt burrito.

"This. I need this."

WILSON WOKE with his body still wrapped around Hildy and his unrelenting erection crushed between them. According to the clock, he still had ten minutes before her alarm would go off. He thought back to Hildy's last words before she fell asleep and could make no better sense of them now than he could the night before. What the fuck was 'this'? God, his cock needed some space before the urge to engage in a little frottage became unbearable. He started to loosen his hold on Hildy, but stopped when she began to moan. He pulled her back in tight, and she immediately settled. He repeated his actions and when he got the same result, he knew what 'this' was. He peppered her neck with tiny kisses. Yeah, he should let her sleep until the alarm went off, but a gentle wake up would be much better for both of them.

"It's time to wake up, sleepy-girl."

Half-asleep, Hildy moaned and complained in gibberish.

"Come on love, it's almost time for the alarm."

"No, want more sleep."

"You can have that later. I want you awake before I get up and make you coffee."

"No. More sleep now."

"Oh, sweetheart, I wish I could grant you that, but I know you have to teach today and the alarm is going off in less than a minute."

"Not fair. I get a nice sleep and poof, gone." Hildy pushed slightly against Wilson's arms and he loosened them, letting her shift around unimpeded.

The alarm blared obnoxiously for a few seconds before

Hildy struck it dumb with a vicious slap. Wilson got out of bed and started dressing. "Time to get moving. You get yourself sorted, I'll get the coffee going and meet you in the kitchen."

Hildy let out a long-suffering sigh. "Okay."

"Good girl. And don't forget your check-list." Wilson just grinned at her sour look, then left.

Wilson had a big mug of coffee waiting on the table for Hildy by the time she entered the kitchen. "What would you like for breakfast?"

"I can get it."

"That wasn't the question. What would you like?" He loved watching her struggle with the urge to refuse him when it was something she really wanted. Ah, the joys of being a Dom.

"Toast, dammit."

"I understand yours isn't the most sunshiny disposition in the morning, but I would appreciate it if you could be polite."

"Toast, please."

"With pleasure." He slipped two slices of bread in the toaster. What would you like on your toast?"

"Butter and honey, please."

"That wasn't so hard, was it? Now, drink your coffee, your toast will be ready in a few minutes."

Wilson left Hildy to a few minutes of quiet reflection. He'd be disrupting it soon enough.

HILDY SAT, quietly sipping her coffee, her mind busy trying to untangle the deluge of overwhelming feelings.

Wilson set the plates of toast on the table, then pulled a sheaf of papers from his pocket and set them in front of her as he sat. "Here's mine. May I have yours?"

Hildy set her cup down and grabbed her own bundle of papers from the chair next to her and slapped them down in the middle of the table. "Here."

Wilson smiled. "Thank you, love. Let me know when you're done."

Hildy grunted and shifted her chair sideways in an attempt to ignore the man who had completely upset her reality. The chuckle she received for her efforts did nothing to improve her mood. She picked up the papers Wilson gave her and started reading.

By the time she reached the second page, her panties were soaked and she knew she was in trouble. So far none of the stuff in his 'I could do this all day every day because it's my favourite thing ever' column turned up on her 'not even if it meant death if I don't' column. She chanced a peek at Wilson. The quirk of his lips and the gleam in his eye was unsettling. Shit, she was in seriously deep trouble. She tried to ignore the uneasy feeling in her belly and the wetness between her legs as she read through to the end. She set her shaking hands in her lap and tried to steady her breathing.

"Done, love?"

Denying it wasn't an option. "Yes."

"Good. Do you have any questions or concerns?"

"Only a shed-load."

Wilson rose and came around to her side of the table and took her hands in his as he crouched. "I should hope so. If it makes you feel any better, so do I."

"It doesn't."

"Would you feel more comfortable if we asked and answered each other in writing?"

"Oh hell, yes."

"Okay. Do you have time before we go to Finn and Macs tonight if we do it by email?"

"I guess."

"Good girl. Now go put on fresh panties and finish getting ready for work. I'll clean up."

How the hell did he know? Hildy tried to ignore her burning face. "I don't understand at all. I thought Doms kept subs to do all the domestic stuff."

"Some do. But, it's not my kink. I'm more of an equitable division of labour kind of guy."

His wink had Hildy's pussy leaking with renewed purpose and she couldn't get away fast enough.

SIX

Wilson waited for Hildy to walk through the door before he followed her in. Finn was hanging her coat and Hildy was kicking off her second boot.

"Everything set, Finn?" Wil asked.

"Yup. Sully and Mac are already downstairs. I'm glad you two finally arrived. She's been baiting him all day."

"I thought he was supposed to go home this morning."

"Since when does Sully do what he's supposed to?"

"Point taken."

By the time they reached the stairs to the playroom, they could hear Mac giving Sully the gears.

"You selfish, miserable fuck. If you aren't capable of playing by the next concert you had better have another oboist handy because I am done. Do you hear me? Done. We had a deal."

"Calm down, Mac."

"Don't you fucking calm down, Mac, me. I kept my end of the deal and more. I don't want to do this any more."

As soon as he reached the bottom of the stairs, Finn spoke up. "Mac. Enough."

"But Finn..."

"Unless you want my tawse on your bare ass right now, enough."

Mac was immediately silent, but anger glowed bright in her eyes.

Wilson took Hildy's hand as they moved to join Sully and Mac in the after-care area. He pulled her down with him as he sat, and arranged her on his lap with her back to his chest so his erection nestled in the seam of her ass. She tried to shift away, but he was ready. He clamped his hands on her hips, and so there was no misunderstanding, he hissed in her ear, "Stay exactly where I put you." She went loose. "Good girl."

Wilson watched as Finn lifted Mac from the sofa and positioned her in much the same way as he had Hildy. The difference was, Mac was naked and Finn had his hands all over her.

With a nod from Wilson, Sully turned to Hildy. "Honey, you did really well last night and we are all so very proud of you. However, you aren't done. You still have two apologies to make and Finn and Mac are here to bear witness. Are you ready?"

Hildy slowly nodded her head, and Wilson took over. "Okay, honey. You will let Sully rub your feet for ten minutes, then you will apologise. Can you do that?"

Having her feet touched was on her check-list as a soft-limit. Not an issue as feet weren't his kink either, but it was the ideal apology to Sully, whose foot fetish was legendary. He'd had a different idea of how her punishment would play out, but after discovering her soft-limits and their earlier email exchanges addressing questions and concerns, he came up with a much better plan.

"I'll try."

"Good girl. Off you go." He placed his hands on her hips and gave a gentle boost to help her on her way. She stood in front of Sully and waited.

"Lay on the sofa and put your feet in my lap. Whatever you do, don't move. Mac will be your worst nightmare if you do anything to delay my return to active duty."

"I'll be good," Hildy replied, as she settled herself as Sully instructed.

Wilson sat for what seemed like the longest ten minutes of his life alternating his gaze between Sully's happy grin and Hildy's angry grimace. The instant the ten minutes were over, he called, "Time."

Sully shifted Hildy's feet off his lap and released them. She sat up and looked him dead in the eye. "Sully, I'm so sorry for not trusting you."

He pulled her close and kissed the top of her head. "You are forgiven, my love. I know deep down you didn't mean it. But I hope you understand that it wasn't something that could be ignored."

"I do."

He kissed her cheek then released her. "Good enough. It's time to go back to Wilson."

Wilson stood, and as Hildy returned, he pulled her in for a tight hug. "Well done, love. You're down to your last apology. Then we can go. Okay?" He felt her nod, but that wasn't enough this time. "I need to hear it, sweetheart."

"Okay."

He sat her on the sofa and settled next to her. "Hildy, I thought long and hard about this, but I've decided to give you five strokes with my leather belt. You'll be over the spanking bench. No trousers, but you may keep your panties on. As long as you can keep still, you may remain unrestrained. After you've taken your five, you may make your apology. Then it's all done and forgotten. If it becomes too much, you still have your safeword. Also, you need to understand, anyone in the room can safeword for you if they think it in your best interest."

"Everyone keeps telling me the sub is in control, but obviously that's not the case if someone else can safeword."

"Honey, sometimes a sub can't safeword. It may be because she's too deep in sub-space. It could be she can't remember what it is, or she can't get the word out. Unfortunately, there are also times where the situation becomes abusive and someone has to step in. There are some subs who refuse to safeword because they don't want to be a wimp. Sound like anybody you know?"

"But if I safeword, I'm done and can't come back." Hildy was near tears.

"If someone else calls red, then we'll talk about it. Remember, you always have yellow. If you need a break, or something needs to change, you can call yellow. And Hildy, safewording is never, ever wimpy. Are we clear?"

"Yes."

"Good. Shall we get started?"

"Okay."

Wilson took Hildy's hand and stood, bringing her to her feet as he rose. "Mac, can you please take Hildy to the spanking bench and get her set up?"

"Sure thing. Come on, Hildy, the sooner we get ready, the sooner this is all done and over with."

Wilson watched Mac lead Hildy away before he turned to Finn and Sully. "I am in over my head with her. She's so fragile and I'm terrified I'm going to do some real damage."

"Oh suck it up, Wil. I already told you, the damage was done years ago. She's comfortable with you. She lets you touch her and hold her without trying to run away like a scalded cat."

"Yeah, about that holding thing. She slept fine when I had my body wrapped around her, but if I tried to let her go, she fussed. Any idea what that's about?" Wilson glanced at the women. They were still getting sorted. He still had a couple of minutes.

"She didn't roll herself up in her quilt?"

"No. When we got into bed, something was bugging her, but she wouldn't tell me what. As soon as I hugged her to me, she fell asleep."

"Yeah, it's a coping thing. Her parents never touched or hugged her. Wrapping herself up in her bedding is how she got through."

"Fuck. And now I have to go beat her ass with my belt."

"Bet she enjoys it."

"I guess we're about to find out."

The men wandered across the room where Mac had Hildy carefully arranged on the spanking bench. She turned as they approached and smiled at Wilson. "She's ready."

"Thanks Mac. Would you mind sitting by her head and giving her some moral support?"

"No problem."

Wilson walked up to the bench and smoothed his hand

down Hildy's back. "Hildy, I'm going to take my belt off and double it over. I want you to understand, at no time will anything but the leather of the strap touch your body. The buckle will be in my hand and I will not do anything to cause you harm. Okay?"

"Okay."

"Alright then. Can you give me a colour? Green if we're good to go, yellow if you need a minute. Red if you're done."

"I'm green."

"Good girl."

Wilson unbuckled his belt making it jingle as loudly as possible before drawing the leather through the loops. He flicked his wrist, snapping the tail as it slipped through the final loop. He wanted Hildy to associate these sounds with anticipation of what would follow.

HILDY BUCKED her hips and kicked wildly as her hands shot back to protect her ass. The blinding pain paralysed her lungs and made her light headed. "Breathe through it honey. It'll pass, I promise." Mac's soothing voice slipped through the foggy chaos in her brain. "Breathe with me. In....and out...in...and out." Hildy slowly regained control and finally started breathing in concert with Mac's steady rhythm.

"Hildy?" Wilson. Between Mac's gentle voice and the deep breathing, she was calm, and she'd almost forgotten. "Hildy, I need you to answer me, love."

She kept her eyes shut. "What?"

"Hildy, look at me."

"I don't want to."

"Now."

Hildy lifted her lids part way and saw nothing but concern on Wilson's face.

"All the way, please." As she did, Wilson bent so they were eye to eye. "We have a problem, love. What I just gave you wasn't much more than a love tap, and you couldn't stay still. What you did was dangerous and if I hadn't been expecting it, I could have caused damage. If we are to continue, I'm going to have to restrain you. Colour?"

Hildy was no quitter and there would be no mistaking the defiance. "Fucking green."

"Hildy, everyone has different tolerances. If it's too much for you, it's okay. It doesn't make you a wimp."

"I am green, dammit."

"Hildy, I'd adjust that attitude if I were you, or you might find yourself sucking on a soap dildo. A little back-talk when we're playing can add to the fun, but it is absolutely unacceptable during punishment."

Hildy's brain finally found some sense of self-preservation. "I'm sorry."

"Forgiven. Colour?"

"I am green, Wil." And she was.

"Okay. I'm going to secure your wrists and ankles in the straps attached to this bench. Once I've done that, I want you to rotate your hands and feet, and wiggle your fingers and toes. If at any point you feel numbness or tingling you must let me know. Use yellow if you really don't want to call the scene, but I need you to understand how very important this is."

While Hildy didn't want to be taken for a wimp, she

knew the difference between taking some pain and risking real damage. "I understand. I promise. Tingling or numbness, I'll call yellow."

Wilson stroked her cheek. "Good girl. I'll also be strapping down your upper back and just below your waist. Once you're secure, I'm going to give you the remaining four stripes fast so it's all done."

Hildy nodded. "Okay." She lay quietly as Wilson set about fastening her to the spanking bench.

"How's that? Any numbness or tingling?"

Hildy rotated her hands and feet, then wiggled her fingers and toes. "I'm good."

"I'll take care of these last two straps and we'll get this over with."

As soon as she felt the strap tighten over her back, Hildy relaxed as calm washed over her.

Wilson noted Hildy's reaction with interest when he buckled the final strap in place over her back. There would be time enough to consider it later. Right now, he had to fulfil his responsibility.

As promised, he finished quickly. He drew his forearm back and flicked his wrist. His belt struck its target, right on her sit-spot. He paused a moment, surprised by Hildy's slow, steady breathing. He glanced around the room. With no apparent concern, he pulled back and repeated the action without further pause until he reached four. He flung his belt to the floor and set about releasing Hildy. He freed her wrists and ankles first. The moment he released the final strap, the one over her back, he covered her with a blanket and pulled her into a tight embrace. "Such a good girl, Hildy."

She looked up at Wilson and smiled. "Wil? I'm really sorry."

"I know. It's done and you're forgiven. Now, let's get you a drink of water and some chocolate."

Wilson lifted Hildy into his arms and carried her to the after-care area and sat down, carefully settling her on his lap. Mac sat next to them with a bottle of water in one hand and some of her special chocolate in the other.

"Here, she deserves the really good stuff."

"Thanks, Mac. I agree."

HILDY'S HAND shook as she held out her house key to Wilson. "I don't think I can do it."

"You had a pretty intense experience, and we're going to have to talk about it."

"I don't know about this whole kinky thing. It seems to be way more talk than sex."

"Communication is key. Yeah, there's lots and lots of talking in the beginning, but as a couple spends more time together, they develop other methods to communicate. Misunderstanding can lead to disaster. It is way better to talk something to death until there is clear understanding, than glossing over it and assuming all parties are on the same channel."

"Kind of like you did with using a safeword if I felt tingling or numbness?"

"Exactly. If I hadn't beat you over the head with how

important that was and you had something start tingling, you would've kept quiet, wouldn't you?"

Hildy's face flamed. "Yeah, I probably would."

"Good girl. Thank you for your honesty." Wilson wrapped his arms around her and she felt peace. "And that's something else I want to talk to you about."

Hildy snuggled deeper. "What?"

"You totally relax when you're wrapped up tight. Whether it's in my arms, in a blanket or strapped down to the spanking bench. When you were unrestrained, you found the light smack of my belt unbearable, yet when I had you strapped tight to the bench, you didn't flinch, no matter how hard I hit you. And each strike was harder than the last. You might have a mark from the last one for a day or two, and I think the ride home gave you a taste of what sitting will be like for a while. If being wrapped is what makes you feel secure, don't worry. I have lots of ideas."

Hildy was embarrassed, but relieved. Wilson had picked up on her need to feel squeezed and didn't judge her.

"One more thing, Hildy. How was your sleep last night?"

Hildy had almost forgotten about the deal she'd made the previous night. The truth was her only option, but she'd promised he could do anything he wanted. She swallowed hard and confessed. "I had a really good sleep."

"Good girl. Your honesty is about to earn you a big reward."

"What are you going to do?"

"Anything I want."

"That's what I was afraid of."

"There's nothing to be afraid of, love. I promise. Only good things tonight."

"Will there be fucking?"

"No more questions, or I might become one of those Doms who demands complete silence from his sub. It's time for bed. I'll lock up and take care of things down here. Go brush your teeth and be waiting on the bed for me. Naked and on your tummy."

As she waited for Wilson to join her, Hildy let her mind wander, ramping up her nervous excitement over what the rest of the evening held for her. She heard him come up the stairs, and her heart sped up as he entered the room.

"Good girls get rewards, and you have been a very good girl."

Hildy found she loved it when Wilson called her a good girl, and realised she would do almost anything to hear him say it.

"What do I have to do to be a good girl, Wil?" She really hoped that didn't sound needy and pathetic.

"Hildy, you're always a good girl. Always. Sometimes you might do naughty things that require punishment, but you are always good."

"But what makes you tell me I'm a good girl?"

"Ah. Usually, I do it as positive reinforcement. Like when I ask you to do something and you do it, or when you tell me the truth, even if you think it's going to get you in trouble. You really like it when I call you good girl, huh?"

Hildy nodded as she buried her face in her quilt. "Good girl. We're going to have to work on using your words to answer questions, though. Part of avoiding miscommunication. I think it's time you got your reward, don't you?"

Hildy nodded with enthusiasm as she let out a muffled, "Yes."

"Such a good girl. Stay just like that. Would my good girl like a nice massage?"

She'd never had one before, but Wilson promised her a reward, so she figured it ought to be something she'd like. She turned her face to the side. "Yes, please."

"Such nice manners deserve to be rewarded, too. Would you like to come, baby girl?"

Baby girl? Hildy was shocked at how the endearment sent her already spasming pussy into overdrive. "Yes, please."

Wilson straddled Hildy, sitting on her thighs, just below the rise of her sore buttocks. "Let's start with a massage."

She heard the pop of a bottle, then felt Wilson's warm, slippery hands gliding along her upper back and working their way over her neck and shoulders. Heaven. He worked his way down her lower back and she groaned in complaint when took his hands away.

"Just need more lube, baby girl."

"Lube? You never said anything about shoving stuff up my ass." Hildy tried to rise, but was stopped by Wilson's hand between her shoulder blades.

"Relax, baby girl. The lube is for your massage. There will be plenty of time in our future to shove stuff up your ass, and I am looking forward to it. In the meantime, all I have planned is a nice massage and an orgasm. Maybe if you're a really good girl, I'll give you two."

Hildy let her upper body go loose, but squeezed her

thighs together at the thought of an orgasm. Or two. It had been quite a long time, and she had no interest in masturbation.

"There you go. Would you like more massage, or would you like your orgasm now?"

"The massage was lovely, but I think I would really like my orgasm."

"If you're not absolutely sure, then I don't think you are ready for your orgasm. Maybe I should just rub your back some more."

"I'm sure, I'm sure. Please, Wil. I want my orgasm."

Wilson chuckled a little. "Well, if you're really sure."

"Please."

"Such lovely manners, baby girl. You just earned yourself that second orgasm." Wilson lifted himself off Hildy. "Turn over, love. Relax your legs and leave them where I put them."

Hildy closed her eyes and gave Wilson control of her body. He spread her legs and bent them so her knees were up and her feet were flat on the mattress. She wanted to come so badly, she didn't dare move.

"It looks like my good girl has a very leaky pussy. I'll mop the mess up in a minute, and I do look forward to plugging that leak very soon. But first, I have two very luscious tits to work over."

Hildy's eyes shot open when her nipples caught fire, and the hiss she tried to hold back quickly became a moan. Her pussy throbbed, and she could feel moisture dribbling towards her asshole. Wilson was grinning at her as he had a nipple trapped between the thumb and forefinger of each hand. He held tight and pulled them up as far as they would go. "That's my very good girl. I had a feeling you'd like this." He pinched and pulled harder. "Would you like to feel my mouth on your nipple, love?"

"Yes please."

"Such pretty manners." Wilson released one nipple before leaning in to tease it with the tip of his tongue. Hildy whined in frustration.

A white flash of pain shot through Hildy as Wil pinched her nipple harder. He lifted his head, his eyes flashing. "Unless you want to learn a lesson in patience, you may want to stop whining and lose the pout. You'll get your orgasms, but only when and how I want to give them." He lowered his head and caught her free nipple hard between his teeth. Her pussy pulsed, and with her nipple dragging through his teeth as he lifted his head, she was close to coming. She frantically tightened her inner muscles, but before they could have any effect, he let go of her nipples.

"Not yet, love. I've already told you, they're mine to give how and when I want, and stealing my pleasure is not a risk you want to take. You'll do well to take my warnings to heart, because you'll only ever get one before an offence becomes punishable." Wilson leaned down and touched his forehead to Hildy's. "For the most part, you've been good, so I won't make you wait too much longer."

Hildy trembled in anticipation as Wilson kissed his way down her body.

"I'm learning all kinds of interesting things about you tonight. Some of them I suspected, but some have been rather pleasant surprises."

Finally. Hildy felt Wilson's fingers spread her outer lips. She used all her willpower to remain still when he dipped his tongue inside her, and she was almost to the breaking point when he kept dragging it upwards in long, slow licks, mercilessly teasing her clit. She thought she might die when he latched on, sucking long and hard, pulling and releasing with a rhythm so intense, when his fingers stroked her g-spot, her world spiralled out of control. When Wilson had wrung out the last whimper of her orgasm and she lay panting with her head floating somewhere near the ceiling, he started the whole process over again.

ONCE HE WAS sure he'd exhausted Hildy's second orgasm, Wilson lifted his head from between her thighs and studied her face. Peace and contentment were written all over it, and his heart squeezed. He slid his way up the bed and settled beside her. Hildy turned to face him, her eyes, glassy. "Thank you."

"It was my pleasure, love."

"How? I'm the only one who came."

"There is more to pleasure than orgasms, love. There are a lot of things that give me sexual pleasure that are not orgasms."

"Like what?"

"The puddle you left on the bed when I did mean things to your nipples, for one."

"You liked that?"

"Honey, I loved that."

"Did you like hitting me with your belt?"

"Yes, and no. I didn't like the reason why I hit you with my belt. I want to be clear, I don't enjoy punishing you. What I did enjoy was having you tied down at my mercy and how drenched your panties were by the time I was done."

"I liked being tied down."

"I know, and I have some ideas about that. In the meantime, I think my good girl is very tired and needs to sleep. Would you like me to wrap you up in your blanket?"

Hildy averted her eyes. "No, it's okay."

"Hildy, look at me." She slowly met his gaze, and he continued, "Either I do it, or you do it. Those are your only options."

Hildy thought for a moment, then whispered. "Would you do it, please?"

Wilson touched his lips to hers. "Of course I will." He gathered up the blanket and wrapped it tightly around her body until only her head poked out. Hildy let out a contented sigh and he was convinced she'd love rope as much as he did. Add the sight of his girl completely immobile, and Wilson's cock was ready to burst. He gathered her in his arms and held her tight, as he kissed her with a passion he hadn't felt in years.

***

HILDY FOUGHT to stay asleep but the light and persistent tickling on her neck made it impossible. She opened her eyes to Wilson watching her. She glanced at the clock and groaned. "It's the middle of the night. What are you doing?"

"Waking my present up to see if she would like to suck my cock before I unwrap and fuck her."

Hildy's heart fluttered, her arousal, instant. "She would, thank you."

Wilson stroked his knuckles along her jawline. "Oh, there are those pretty manners again."

In an instant, Hildy was on her back with her head hanging off the edge of the bed and Wilson's cock tapping her lips.

"What a gorgeous sight. Open."

In this position, Hildy knew what Wilson wanted, so she parted her lips and relaxed her throat, her tongue extended in invitation. Self-preservation had perfected her ability to swallow cock. She'd had more than her fair share of men grab her hair and plant their balls on her chin in a single thrust. She'd learned quickly to anticipate and plan accordingly.

Wilson settled his bent knees either side of Hildy's head and slid his cock along her tongue, pulling back before he got anywhere near her throat. He slid in again and held still. "Close your mouth and suck like the good girl you are."

Good girl. Hildy didn't think she would ever tire of hearing those words. She closed her mouth and tried to shift her head to accept more of him. "Don't. Move." Hildy continued to suck, but held her head still. "You'll take what I give you. Nothing more."

Hildy was confused. Here she was in the perfect position to take a whole cock down her throat, and the man had given her barely more than the head. She did the best she could with what she had to work with, and almost sighed with relief when Wilson started pumping his hips. Each thrust, a little deeper until he finally reached the entrance to her throat. She wanted all of him, and she opened her throat as wide as she could, hoping he'd take the hint.

"That's very generous of you sweetheart, but not this time. As much as I'd love to feel my cock deep in your throat, it will never happen when biting is the only meaningful way you could tell me to stop. Suck just a little more, then I think I'll be ready to unwrap you."

Hildy continued to suck, alternating between strong and gentle, savouring his taste, but wanting more. She wanted to tease him, lap up the drops of pre-cum with the tip of her tongue, but his movements made it impossible. He was right, she would take what he gave her.

So caught up in what she was doing, Wilson's cock was almost clear of her lips by the time Hildy realised he wasn't going to give her anymore. She fought the urge to whine. She'd been warned. Wilson's hand slipped behind her head, gently lifting it as he resettled her on the bed. He dropped a kiss on her forehead, then retrieved a condom from his trousers.

Wilson peppered her face and neck with feather-light kisses as he suited up. "Mmm, that was lovely, and I look forward to more very soon, but I have another warm, wet place in mind to bury my cock." Wilson's words had Hildy feeling more than warm and wet. Her muscles were clenching rhythmically as she struggled to control her errant mouth.

Wilson chuckled while he slowly loosened the blanket. "Your lips may not be telling me to just fucking get on with it, but your eyes sure are. In my family, we always unwrap gifts slowly and carefully so we can reuse the wrapping."

"I don't think you need to worry too much about this tearing."

"True, but it's a good habit, so I think I'll stick with it."

Hildy fought hard to hold in her frustration, but based

on her experience so far, patience did seem to have its rewards.

"Ah, I do believe you've figured it out. Good girl."

Hildy felt the cool air hit her hot skin as Wilson finally removed the last layer of blanket. She reached up and stroked his face. He smiled, then took her hands in his and settled them above her head. "Leave them there, love." Hildy nodded, not trusting her voice. She wanted this so badly, she didn't want to do or say anything to fuck it up. "Good girl. Now spread your legs wide. I need to taste you before I fuck you."

His words had Hildy on edge. Then his tongue started lapping at her pussy, and just when she thought she might go over the edge, he stopped. "Not yet, love. You don't get to come until I decide it's time." He gave her pussy one long lick then lifted and closed her legs before resting them on his left shoulder.

On his knees, with his cock firmly in hand, Wilson guided it into Hildy's weeping pussy, savouring each delicious inch. When his flesh was finally flush with hers, he hugged her legs to him with both arms, using them as an anchor while he savagely pistoned his cock in and out of her body. He watched her face the whole time, waiting until he knew she was almost of out of patience before leaning forward, trapping her legs between them. "Good girl. You can come when you like. I'll be right behind you."

He was almost at the tipping point, but her long, deep moan was all it took for him to put his impending orgasm on hold and slam his hips into over-drive, rolling and pounding, doing everything he could to keep her coming. When she was in the final spasms, he buried his head in the crook of her neck and moaned as he filled her with everything he had.

He lifted his head and beamed with pride at her determined obedience. "Such a good girl, Hildy. Your hands are precisely where they should be. Good girls get rewards." He carefully withdrew from her body, lowering her legs in the process. "I'm going to go take care of the condom, then come back to take care of you. Don't move a muscle."

WILSON'S VOICE sounded far away, but she heard him clearly calling her a good girl for not moving her arms. It took everything she had to keep them still during the longest, most intense orgasm of her life, but she did it, and now there would be a reward.

What kind of reward? Orgasm? She might need days to recover from the one she just had. Was it just one? There had been a point where she worried Wilson might make it go on forever.

"Are you ready for your reward?" Wilson flashed her that wicked grin of his and she was reduced to a puddle on the bed.

"I think it depends on what it is."

"It's not an orgasm this time."

Hildy was surprised at herself. She never thought she'd see the day where she would even consider turning down an orgasm, let alone one of the mind-blowing kind Wilson was clearly capable of providing. "What then?"

"Close your eyes, baby girl."

Hildy let her eyelids fall. Her sudden exhaustion over-powered her temptation to peek. "Good girl."

The next thing she knew, she was being cocooned. The fabric was much, much softer than her quilt, and she moaned as Wilson wrapped it snugly around her bare flesh.

"You can open them, now."

Hildy forced her eyes open and looked down at the fluffy purple blanket enveloping her body and grinned. "For me?"

"Yes, for you, love."

"To keep?"

"Yes, to keep."

Hildy fought back the tears. Nobody but Sully and her uncle ever gave her gifts. "Thank you."

Wilson reached over to turn off the light. "You are most welcome, love. Sleep now." She nuzzled against his chest and let out a contented sigh as he wrapped himself around her.

SEVEN

Wilson picked up the phone for what must have been the tenth time in as many minutes. This time, he pressed the final digit and let the call connect.

"Hey Wil, what's up?"

"I wanted to know if you would like to come to Finn and Mac's with me tonight?"

"I don't know. Things didn't go so well last time I went."

"Remember what Mac and I told you? All is forgiven, clean slate, and no bringing up past transgressions."

"Easier said than done, you know."

"I know, but the fear will just keep getting bigger if you don't deal with it now."

"Who's going to be there?"

"I can tell you Sloan won't be there. Does that help?"

"Not really."

"We don't have to go, but if we do and you can't deal, just safeword, okay."

"I'm too embarrassed."

"I can understand that, and I'm sure as hell not going to try to tell you how to feel, but I would really like it if you would give it a try. You know that's all I'll ever ask of you."

"But what if someone brings up what happened last time?"

"Won't happen."

"How can you be sure?"

"Trust."

"It's not that simple."

"For me, it is. You need to decide whether you trust me enough to keep you safe or not. I'm still earning your trust, and it's okay if you're not there yet, baby girl."

"I do trust you to keep me safe, it's the unknowns that I can't trust."

"I get that, but trusting me to keep you safe is trusting me to take care of the unknowns."

"It's too scary."

"You have safewords for that. If it's really that much too scary, you should call red right now. Are you calling red?"

"No, dammit."

"Brave girl. How about we go early and have supper with Finn and Mac, then we can see if you can relax enough to stay. If not, we can leave before anyone else arrives?"

"We can't just invite ourselves to supper."

"We didn't. They offered it up as an option if we'd like to join them. They're ordering in, so no need for advanced notice. So, what do you say?"

"And we can leave before people arrive if I'm not up for it?"

"Red, and we're out of there, I promise."

"Okay."

"I'm proud of you, baby girl. I'll be there at five. Bring your blanket and whatever you need for over-night. We're sleeping at my place."

"But we always sleep at my house."

"So far, we've always slept at your house. Tonight, that changes. I'll see you soon."

"Fine." Click.

Grumpy girl. He could work with that.

"You're really not mad at me?"

Wilson gathered Hildy into his arms. "I'm proud of you."

"I don't get it. How can you be proud of me for safe-wording out of staying for the play party?"

"It's another layer of trust between us. You trust me enough to respect your safeword and I trust you enough to use it appropriately."

"How do you know I didn't use it as an excuse to leave?"

"Back to your face showing everything, baby girl. I knew we weren't staying long before you called red. Would you like the ten cent tour?"

"Yes please."

Wilson took Hildy's hand and led her through each room of his house, leaving his bedroom for last.

"It's still early, are you willing to try a bit of rope-play before we head to bed?"

"What kind of rope-play?"

"Nothing too complicated, but a little more intricate than the gauntlets I did on Mac at the last play-party."

"I don't know."

"How about I show you some pictures and video of what I want to do so you have a better idea of what to expect?"

"Okay."

"Good, I'll be right back." Wilson shot out of the room and returned with his laptop a minute or so later. He sat on the bed next to Hildy and clicked through the file directory until he opened a folder called 'Body Harness Tutorial' and set up a slow slide-show. "I use these photos when I teach a class. This first one is of the end result. The next bunch show the steps to get there, and the last bunch are of the more elaborate rigging that can be done once the basics are mastered. If you have any questions, concerns, or want a longer look at a photo, tap my arm. Shall we begin?"

Hildy nodded. "Okay."

Wilson started the slide show and watched Hildy's face carefully as each picture slid across the screen.

<hr>

HILDY COULDN'T BELIEVE what she was seeing. It was a wearable hug and oh, how she wanted one. "This is what you want to do tonight?"

"If you're game, I do."

Hildy could barely contain her excitement. "Oh, I'm game. What happens next?"

"You watch the demo video while I go grab my gear.

After that, we begin. Normally, you'd be naked, but I don't want to overwhelm you, so you'll remain clothed."

Hildy nodded, returning her attention to the laptop. She barely registered Wil's exit as she sat captivated by the activity on the screen.

By the time Wilson returned, Hildy had played the video four times. Well, not the whole thing. She just repeated the part where Wilson does the actual binding and mentally inserted herself as the model.

Wilson brushed a finger down Hildy's arm. "So, are you ready to make that fantasy a reality?"

Hildy's earlier bravado was instantly replaced with mortification as she felt like a nun caught in the condom aisle. She buried her chin in her chest and felt the burn rise to the tops of her ears. "Um..."

Wilson slipped a finger beneath Hildy's chin and tilted her face up. "Hey now, there's nothing to be embarrassed about, love. We all have fantasies, and I couldn't wish for better than a woman who fantasises about receiving what I like to dish out."

Hildy tried to turn her head, but Wilson latched onto her chin and held it in place while he brushed his lips over hers. "Change of plans, love. You're not ready for this just yet. Be naked by the time I get back."

Hildy stared at the floor and silently berated herself for being so utterly ridiculous. She had the perfect opportunity to try something she could wear anytime, anywhere, that could potentially provide the safe feeling she got from being wrapped in a blanket and she blew it.

"Were my instructions somehow not clear?"

Hildy startled and lifted her gaze to Wilson's. His eyes lacked their usual sparkle. "Huh?"

"Your manners have slipped considerably. That's not a particularly polite response. Would you like to try again?"

Wilson may have worded it as a request, but from the tone of his voice, it was an order, and she'd best comply before she landed herself in an even bigger pile of shit. No matter how badly she wanted to return her gaze to the floor, she toughed it out and maintained eye-contact. "Um, pardon?"

"Marginally better. When I left, I told you to be naked by the time I returned. You are still dressed, and I would like to understand why. Perhaps you'd care to explain?"

Hildy already had hold of a chunk of hair at the base of her skull before she caught herself and snatched her hand away, slipping it, along with her other hand beneath her thighs.

"Stop. What was that about?"

Hildy looked up and glared at Wilson. Fuck! She was an emotional teeter-totter and the urge to run away was overwhelming. This was why she didn't do relationships. Why hadn't she just stuck to her usual routine of bang and bounce where there were no expectations beyond getting off?

Wilson crouched in front of Hildy and laid his hands on her knees. "I'm going to help you get undressed and wrap you in your blanket; then we'll talk."

"I can undress myself."

Wilson stood and stepped to the side. "Okay. I'll give you ten seconds to get on it."

Hildy grabbed the hem of her top and whipped it over her head, firing it across the room when she let go. She'd pick it up later. She didn't want to give him any reason to undress her, that would be too intimate. She stole a quick glance at Wilson as she unhooked her bra, but his face gave nothing away. She returned her focus to removing her clothing. She needed the calm and safety of her blanket, and the sooner she got naked, the sooner she would get it. Except, would she? Wil said they were going to talk.

EIGHT

"DAMMIT, Mac, I don't know how to deal with this." Hildy paced up and down the length of her living room as she tried to adequately articulate her dilemma over the phone. "I'm so fucking mixed up." She let go of the hank of hair before she tugged hard enough to pull it out. She needed to pay closer attention to what she was doing before it became a problem again.

"Sweetie, we're all mixed up to varying degrees. Life is messy. It's how we deal with that mess that counts. So let's figure out how we can work with your mess, shall we?"

"I don't know. Things get scary, and I'm ready to walk away, then something wonderful happens, and I'm not so sure."

"Oh, honey, I know that feeling. I get the urge to flee back to my place regularly. I've come really close a few times, but Finn has managed to talk me down. Tell me what happened."

"The short version is, Wil was going to do a rope harness on me, and I was totally on board, until I wasn't."

"Short version? That's barely a tweet. Can you give me a little more to work with?"

"I don't know what went wrong. Wilson tried to talk to me about it afterwards, but I couldn't explain something I don't understand myself. I still can't"

"That's fair enough. Do you want to try the rope harness?"

"I'm cool with the idea of it. The reality of it is what I'm not so sure about."

"Is it possible you freaked because you were alone with Wilson?"

Hildy thought for a moment. "I don't know. Maybe."

"I know you aren't ready to play at a party yet, but what if you had some moral support? Finn and I would be happy to help out, but if you're not comfortable with us, I'm sure Sully would—"

"No! Not Sully. I don't think I could be naked around him just yet."

"You wouldn't have to be naked, you could—"

"Look, it's one thing for Sully and me to have in-depth conversations about our sexual escapades, but actually being present for them is something I'm going to have to work my way up to."

"Yeah, I get that. What about having Finn and me being there for you?"

Hildy noticed the small clump of hair and bloody skin in her hand a split second before she felt the pain in her scalp. Maybe she didn't have this as under control as she thought.

"Hildy? Are you there?"

"Shit. Yeah, sorry." Hildy frowned as she continued to

stare at the hair in her hand. "Um, you and Finn being there..."

"Hildy, what's going on? Are you okay?"

"Yeah, yeah, I'm fine. Just a bit distracted."

"How about this? You come over for supper. I'll call Wil and invite him to come with his gear and we'll just let the evening unfold. No pressure."

"Okay, I think I can do that. Thanks, Mac."

"You are most welcome. We'll eat at six, so how about you swing by around five-thirty?"

"Sure, sounds good. I'll see you then."

"See ya."

Hildy dropped the phone and let the tears fall. She thought she was done with this shit. She couldn't remember the last time she'd resorted to hair pulling. She checked her watch. Less than half an hour until the next student and she needed to get her shit together.

———

"Hey, Mac, I was thinking about calling you."

"About what happened with Hildy last night?"

"Yeah, but I'm glad she's already talked to you. She had me pretty worried."

"She didn't really give me any details. All I know for sure is she's feeling pretty messed up. Something happened while we were talking and she became really distracted."

"Maybe I should call Sully."

"I think you should hold off on that. For now, anyway. Her relationship with Sully is changing, and she needs to process it in her own way. She's coming over for supper tonight. I told her I would invite you and your gear along and we'd see how things work out. Just the four of us and no pressure. Are you up for that?"

"Sure. What kind of gear did you have in mind?"

"Whatever you like, but you might want to make sure there's rope in your arsenal."

Wilson chuckled. "Honey, there's *always* rope in my arsenal."

"I know, but I figured I'd mention it anyway, just to be sure."

"And I appreciate that. Is there anything else I can bring tonight?"

"Nope, just your lovely self and your gear. Supper's at six. I told Hildy to be a half hour early, but I think you should already be here when she arrives."

"Will do. Is Finn around?"

"Yeah, he's right here."

<hr>

HILDY WAS self-conscious about the wound on her scalp and had struggled all evening to keep her hands away from her head, desperate to avoid drawing any attention to it. Something she was finding harder to do once she and Mac and retired to the living room after supper. At least while they were eating, she'd had something to keep her hands occupied. Now her nerves were getting the better of her, and to fight the urge to pull more hair out, she squeezed her hands into fists so tight, her neatly trimmed nails dug into her palms.

"Hildy, are you okay?"

Mac's question broke her concentration, and her hand

shot to the sore spot on her head. "What? Yeah, fine. Just a bit nervous."

"I can understand that, especially since I think those two are up to something."

"What do you mean?"

"After I invited Wil for supper, he and Finn had a long, private conversation. When Finn threatened a week without orgasms if I got within earshot one more time, I figured it was time to give up trying to find out what they were up to."

"Maybe it's time I should go."

Mac made a sad puppy-dog face. "And leave me to face the unknown by myself?"

Hildy snorted. "Oh, come on, Mac. This shit is nothing new to you."

"Yeah, this shit, as you call it, is nowhere near as new to me as it is to you, but there is still an awful lot of unknown and scary out there for me. I do think they're up to something, and knowing Finn, it's going to push my boundaries. I understand if you need to leave, and I can respect that, but if you can bring yourself to stay, even if you red-light out of whatever Wil has up his sleeve, I would really appreciate the moral support."

And that was it, there was no way Hildy could leave now. Mac had been so wonderful and supportive, right from that first phone call. "Okay, I'll stay."

Mac got up and sat next to Hildy on the sofa and pulled her in for a big hug. "Thanks, sweetie."

"So that's why we got relegated to kitchen-elves, Wil, Mac wanted a little alone time with Hildy."

Hildy stiffened as she tried to pull away, but Mac hugged her tighter before gently releasing her. "Relax, he's teasing. Although, I'm sure he'd be all for me participating in a little girl on girl action, it would never happen without his permission."

Hildy looked up in time to see Finn wink at Wil. "Damn straight, love. But not tonight. We've got other plans."

Mac smiled and patted Hildy's knee. "See, I told you they were up to something." Then she turned to Wil, her voice tinged with steel. "I think it would be a really good idea for you two to tell us what your intentions are now."

Hildy held her breath and fisted her hands again, worried Mac was heading for punishment.

"Calm down, Mac. Wil and I were hoping you and Hildy might be willing to let us rig you up in chest harnesses. Nothing elaborate, and nothing you haven't done before. We thought maybe it might work better for Hildy if she had some company. Wil and I are going to go to the music room and deal with some administrative stuff while you two discuss this. Come get us when you're done." Without another word, he and Wil left the room.

Mac turned back to face Hildy. "So, are you feeling brave?"

"No."

"What are you scared of?"

"Failure."

"Remember that conversation we had before that play party you came to? The one where I said all anyone should ask of you is to try?"

"Yeah."

"Then, if you try, how can you fail?"

"By not actually doing whatever it is I've been asked to try."

"Really? If you agree to try something, you give it a go, but don't finish because it's not for you for whatever reason, is that failing?"

"Of course it is."

"Okay, let me ask you this, if Finn asked me to try play piercing and I did, but safe-worded because it was more than I could stand, have I failed?"

"Of course not."

"Why?"

"Because you tried, just like he asked."

"Now, what makes you any different from me?"

"It doesn't matter."

Mac looked at Hildy's fisted hands. "Honey, you're going to do some damage like that. Let me have a look."

"No, they're fine"

"Either you let me look, or I'm going to yell for those men, and I can assure you, if I yell, Finn will come through here like the devil is on his ass. Now, do you want to deal with me, or a couple of over-protective Domly-types?"

Hildy eased open her hands as she squeezed her eyes shut.

"Oh, sweetie, you've almost broken the skin. We need to find you another way to cope"

"This is my other way to cope." Hildy really needed to regain control of her mouth from her subconscious.

Mac gathered Hildy in her arms before shouting, "Wil!"

Hildy tried to pull away, but Mac was strong even as she soothed. "I'm sorry, sweetie, but I like you too much to let you hurt yourself."

Finn and Wil burst into the room and Wil immediately

dropped to the floor in front of Mac and Hildy. "What happened?"

"She's been self-harming. Look at her palms."

Hildy was mortified. Trapped as she was, she buried her face in Mac's neck and tried to hide her hands.

Wil stroked her leg. "Love, I need to see your hands."

"Red."

And with that one little word, Mac released her and she was free. She jumped up, ready to race for the door when she caught sight of the tears rolling down Mac's cheeks. Fuck! The last thing she wanted to do was hurt her friend. Damn Uncle Erich for dying. Ever since that fucking funeral, her life just kept getting more and more complicated. She cast one more wistful look at the door, then heaving a big sigh, she dropped her chin, and held her hands out to Wil.

Wil took her hands in his and kissed each palm gently before pulling her in for a hug. "Oh, sweetie. What could be so bad that you'd hurt yourself?"

Hildy burrowed her face into Wil's chest and struggled not to clench her fists or reach up for a hank of hair.

Mac spoke for her. "She's worried about failing you, Wil."

Wil hugged Hildy tighter to him and kissed the top of her head. "Even if you did fail me, what's the very worst thing that could happen?"

Hildy squeezed her eyes shut and tried to block out how failure had been dealt with in her family. The everyday careless indifference was bad enough, but it was the wilful neglect she endured for failure that spawned the hair pulling. The worst that could happen for failing Wil? He could walk away.

NINE

EARLY MORNING LIGHT filtered through the gap in the curtains in Finn and Mac's spare room, and Wil stroked Hildy's hair as she slept in his arms. To say the evening had been emotionally charged was understatement. He was oblivious to so much about Hildy and her past, and he was powerless to help her until he had a better handle on what she was dealing with. He suspected even Sully didn't understand the full extent of the damage.

The plan for the night before had been to keep the subject matter light and transition into some simple rope bondage. He'd known at supper things weren't going to go as planned. As hard as Hildy tried to hide it, her face was broadcasting her struggle in HD and they'd spent enough time together over the past weeks for him to know this self-harm thing probably wasn't new.

What the fuck was he doing wrong? There was no question she liked the idea of bondage. He wrapped her up like a mummy every fucking night before they went to sleep, and she was more than good with it. The squirming she so desperately tried to hide when she saw others all roped up was further evidence of her interest. So why was it whenever he brought the rope out, she lost it? Blanket bondage was all well and good for blow-jobs, but it didn't lend itself well to much of anything else he enjoyed.

Perhaps he could come up with a gradual transition from blanket to rope. He continued to stroke Hildy's hair as he considered his options. It didn't take him long to come up with an action plan with options dependent on Hildy's reactions. He kissed the top of her head and gave her a gentle squeeze. "Wake up, sleepyhead, it's time to get up, and I smell coffee."

"Five more minutes." Hildy whined and snuggled deeper into Wilson's embrace.

After one more squeeze, Wilson pulled away and unwrapped Hildy's blanket. "Nope, it's time to get up. We've got a busy day ahead."

"How's that? We didn't make any plans for today." Hildy stretched her arms above her head, then rubbed her eyes. "What if I already have plans?"

"Do you?"

"Well, no. But I could have."

"No more talking. You're too grumpy before you've had coffee." Wilson climbed out of bed and got dressed. He grabbed Hildy's clothes and laid them on the bed for her. "Here, put these on. We'll have coffee here, then go back to your place to get showered and clean clothes. I'll have your coffee ready for you by the time you get to the kitchen." He turned and left, not waiting for a response. He considered Hildy's pre-coffee grumpiness. Yes, it could be frustrating, but it's part of who she was, so he would work around it.

DAMN HE WAS BOSSY. Why the hell did she put up with it? Life had been so much easier when she didn't have a man in it. What right did he have to make plans for her day without discussing them first, anyway?

Hildy got up and made the bed before slipping into her clothes. She picked up her blanket and held it to her face a moment before shaking it out to fold it. She reconsidered and hurled it on the bed. She was getting too attached. One stupid present and she was ready to change the way she lived her life?

She needed to get the fuck out, now. She gathered her belongings and took one last, wistful look at the blanket, then slipped out of the bedroom. For once luck was on her side, she could hear Wil, Mac, and Finn in the kitchen. She tip-toed her way to the front door, pausing only long enough to slide into her shoes and snag her coat off the hook.

The deadbolt was well-oiled and opened without a sound. As soon as she was outside, Hildy twisted the door-knob to keep the latch from snapping as she eased the door closed. So far, so good. She raced to her car, thankful she'd parked on the street. She wouldn't have to waste valuable time backing out of the driveway.

Once she was safely away, coffee was her first priority. She considered going to Sully's, but solitude was more appealing. She'd had enough of bossy men for a while. Her phone rang and at the next stop light, she turned it off without bothering to check who had called. She didn't care. Dammit, chances were good someone, probably Wil, would show up at her house before too long, and she wasn't up for that yet. She spotted a coffee shop and pulled into the parking lot.

Yeah, this would do for a few hours. She could happily spend a lazy morning loading up on caffeine while reading magazines. Anything to take her mind of her fucked up life for a while.

Hours later, Hildy had exhausted the magazine selection and moved on to the newspapers. As she idly flipped the page, she almost spilled her coffee. There, in the middle of the entertainment section, was a two-page spread on her uncle. Blinking back tears, she closed the paper, and abandoned her coffee. She thought she had her grief under control, but seeing the photographs brought it flooding back.

She managed to hold herself together long enough to drive home, but by the time she got there, she was too distraught to notice her parents until she was out of her car and it was too late.

WIL RANG the doorbell and knocked again. "Hildy, love, I'm worried. Please open the door." He tried to stay calm. He'd alternated between angry and worried sick all day. Between Sully's call about her bat-shit crazy parents being on the rampage and Hildy not responding, he was firmly entrenched in worried sick. Fuck. He knew he should have listened to his gut and headed straight to Hildy's the moment he discovered her gone instead of listening to Mac's advice to give her some space.

The silence on the other side of the door was making him crazy. "Hildy, please, just let me know you're okay."

More silence. He looked at his watch and said, "That's it, if you don't open this door and show me you're okay within the next sixty seconds, I am going to call 911 and have the police come to do a welfare check."

He heard the locks click and sighed with relief as the door creaked. Hildy's eye appeared in the narrow opening. "I'm fine, now go away."

Wilson stuck out his foot to keep her from closing the door. "Honey, what little I can see of you doesn't look fine. Can I please come in and see for myself?"

"No, I'm fine. I just want to be alone."

"Fair enough. When I see that you are fine, I'll go away. I'm not the only one who's worried about you, though. Sully is frantic, and there is no way I am going to face Mac without being able to tell her I saw you with my own two eyes."

Hildy huffed, and when she opened the door, Wilson had to stomp on his rage. She'd made a valiant effort with the make-up, but there was no mistaking the black eye and split lip.

Fuck, when Sully had asked him to come over to check on her, he'd only said things might get ugly and she would likely be upset. Either Sully's idea of upset was a far cry from his own, or Sully had seriously underestimated the situation. Both options sucked.

God, there were so many things running through his head at that moment, and most of them involved extreme violence, but his number one priority had to be Hildy, and she was hurt.

"There, now you can go report back to the others that I'm fine and want to be left alone."

"Baby girl, what I see does not even come close to qualifying as fine." Wilson stepped through the door, and fought his urge to take Hildy into his arms. She'd just been assaulted, and she needed to be able to trust him. "Honey, let's get some ice on your poor face."

"It shows?" Hildy asked, the disappointment clear in her tone.

Wilson nodded and headed to the kitchen to get something to help with the swelling. He needed some time to get himself together. He needed to be strong for her, and he didn't trust his voice just yet.

It took a minute of rooting around the freezer before he found a small, unopened bag of frozen peas. Perfect. He turned to see Hildy in the doorway, looking so lost and fragile. He held out the package. "Go get comfy in the living room and put this on your face. I'll be there soon."

As soon as Hildy was out of sight, Wilson pulled out his phone and called Mac. "Hey, it's Wil."

"It's about fucking time you called, you inconsiderate jerk."

"Take it easy, she only just let me in, and that was after threatening to call the cops. Look, it got uglier than Sully led me to believe. I haven't had a chance to fully check her over, but she tried to cover up facial injuries with make-up and I need some advice on how to clean her up as painlessly as possible."

"If she has make-up, then she's probably got wipes to remove it. Go have a look in her bathroom. How bad is it?"

"From what I can tell, time and TLC should take care of it. I'll know better once I get that make-up off. I'll let you know right away if I think she needs medical attention, otherwise, assume no news is good news."

"Okay. I'll let everyone else know you're with her and not to worry. You take care of her and let her know we're here if she needs us."

"Will do. Thanks, Mac." Wil disconnected. It didn't take him long to locate the wipes and when he saw the bottle of Tylenol, he took that too. She had to be hurting. As he passed through Hildy's bedroom, he grabbed her quilt.

He entered the living room and Hildy looked up, the left side of her face obliterated by the bag of peas. "Hey, baby girl, we can talk later, but right now, let's get you fixed up." Wil laid the quilt across the arm of the sofa, pulled a wipe out of the packet, and crouched in front of Hildy. "We need to get that make-up off your face, but it's probably going to hurt. Have you taken anything for the pain?"

"I'm fine."

"That's not what I asked, love."

"No, I don't need anything."

"In case you change your mind." Wilson set the bottle on the table and held up the wipe. "I need to assess your injuries, so let's start with your face. Can you move the bag of peas so we can get you cleaned up and I can have a good look?"

Hildy brought her knees to her chest. "It's nothing that a little time can't heal."

"You're probably right, but I want to make sure."

Hildy lowered the bag from her face and Wilson carefully schooled his expression. Hildy was upset enough without his anger making it worse. "Close your eyes and hold still. I'll be as quick as I can." He reached up and started at her brow, surprised and relieved at how effectively the wipe worked. He worked his way around her eye, tamping his anger harder every time she winced. "Okay, love, almost done. I just need to do your eyelid." He pulled a fresh wipe from the packet and carefully slid it across her bruised flesh.

"It's pretty swollen, but I think you're right, time will take care of it. Where else are you hurt?"

"Just my face."

"Truth?"

"Really, Wil. It's just my face. I'm fine, so you can go now."

"Not a chance, love. You seem a little shocky to me. Let's get you all bundled up, then I'll make you some broth."

"Just go. I don't want you to bundle me up, and I'll get my own food when I feel like it." Hildy put the peas back to her face and turned her head away.

"Hildy, look at me." Seconds ticked by. Finally, Hildy turned back to face him and he smiled. "There you are. Honey, I'm not going anywhere. I'm not walking away. We've had this discussion before about the difference between want and need."

Wilson rose, picked up the blanket, and unfolded it. "Up you get." Hildy stood and laid the packet of peas on the coffee table. He held the blanket open and gently wrapped it around her as she stepped into it. Once she was swaddled, he carefully lifted her into his arms, and laid her on the sofa. He tucked a cushion beneath her head and settled the peas back on her battered face. "There you go, love. I'll be back in a few minutes."

As the broth heated in the microwave, failure and guilt tangled with helplessness and weighed heavy in Wilson's gut. It was all his fault his sweet, sweet Hildy was hurt.

He'd pushed too hard, and when she'd left, he didn't go after her. He should have been here, protected her. God, his heart hurt. The microwave beeped. Time to go fight for his woman.

"Here you go, love." Wilson set the cup on the coffee table. He reached down and removed the bag of peas, then helped Hildy sit up. "Comfy?"

"I can't feed myself like this."

Wilson picked up the cup and held the straw to Hildy's lips. "You don't need to. You just need to be comfy. Open." Hildy sighed, opened her mouth, sucked in a mouthful, and swallowed. "Good girl. I'm going to go pop those peas back in the freezer, then you can have the rest."

When Wilson returned, Hildy's head was resting against the back of the sofa, her eyes closed. He wanted to bundle her into his arms and never let her go. He eased down next to her and waited for her to open her eyes. "Ready for more?" She nodded, and he replaced the straw at her lips, holding it steady for her to sip at her leisure.

The straw gurgled as Hildy sucked the final drops of broth through it. She pulled her head back and gave him a half smile. "Thank you."

Her first smile since he'd arrived. "You're welcome, love." A glimmer of hope squeezed past fear and now he had to risk its retreat. "We have to talk about what happened today, and sooner is better than later." Hildy lowered her chin to her chest. "How about, for now, I talk, you listen?" Hildy nodded.

"I want to start with this morning. I need you to under-stand that I am not angry with you. I pushed you too hard, to the point where you felt the need to quietly disappear. I'm sorry. I'm even sorrier that I didn't come after you. I wanted to, but Mac said you probably needed some space, and I should give it to you. I shouldn't have listened to her."

Hildy looked up. "No, she was right. I spent the morning and part of the afternoon in a coffee shop avoiding you. I'd probably still be there but..." She trailed off and dropped her chin again.

Wilson forced himself to back off. Pushing her was what had got him into this fucking mess in the first place. "Alright, love. It's been a rough day, and you need some rest. We'll leave the rest for now and I'll take you to bed."

"No, just get me out of this quilt and leave."

Fuck, he was losing it. Losing her. "Hildy," Wilson's voice broke, "God, Hildy, I can't. I know it's selfish of me, but I can't leave you by yourself. Going all day not knowing where you were or if you were safe was bad enough, but seeing you hurt ripped my fucking heart out. I need to know you're safe. If you really need me to go, I'll get Sully to —"

"No, I definitely can't deal with Sully right now."

Wil took a long shuddering breath and pulled himself together. "Sweetheart, it's been a shitty day and we both need sleep. I'll sleep out here on the sofa, but I want to get you settled in your bed first. I'll unwrap you so you can get yourself ready, then I'll bundle you back up before you go to sleep, okay?"

"I don't have any choice, do I?"

"Not when it comes to being here by yourself, no."

"Fine. Can you unwrap me please?"

Wilson helped Hildy to her feet and carefully removed the quilt. He was dying to kiss her, but didn't dare. Even if she were open to it, he'd be too scared of hurting her. As soon as she was free, she took off towards her bedroom, not even glancing back. He sank onto the sofa and buried his face in his hands.

How did her life get so complicated? Hildy stared at her bruised face in the mirror as she tried to find the most painless way to brush her damn teeth. What a mess. Why the hell hadn't this perfectly nice guy, who cooks and could fuck for bloody England, given up on her already? She was fucking neurotic, wouldn't let him tie her up, even though they both fucking well wanted it. What was wrong with her? He should be out finding himself a bloody normal woman, not some stupid—

"What have I told you about that?"

Shit. She caught his reflection in the mirror. God, he looked awful. Had she done that? She'd been so self-absorbed, she didn't notice him arrive. She spit out the toothpaste and carefully rinsed her mouth. "What?"

"You know exactly what, baby girl."

Yeah, he was going to make her ass pay dearly for putting herself down. "You wouldn't, would you?"

"While you're injured? Of course not. Save them up for when you're better? Without a doubt. Are you ready to go to bed now?"

Hildy turned, avoiding Wil's sad eyes as she nodded. Bed and sleep, that's what she needed. Fuck. It had been weeks since she'd slept by herself, weeks in which she'd woken feeling well-rested, where she'd felt safe and loved. What kind of idiot would give that up?

"Hildy, enough. Now, scoot."

Eyes firmly fixed on the floor, Hildy trudged to the bed. She was angry with herself for the hasty choices she'd made. A fit of pique, and if she were totally honest with herself, fear, had led her down the path to misery. Was Wil really here because he cared about her, or was it because he felt responsible? Shit. She didn't want to sleep alone, but she didn't want him to sleep with her out of some misguided sense of obligation.

By the time she reached the bed, Wilson was sitting on it. He patted his lap and opened his arms wide. "Come sit down, love."

She hesitated for a moment, but it had been a lifetime since he'd held her and the need to be in his arms overwhelmed her doubt and fear. She eased down and leaned into Wilson's chest, sighing when he held her close. She let the silence settle for a few minutes before she gave in to her need to know. "Why are you here?"

Wilson tipped her chin up and gazed into her eyes before placing a gentle kiss on the corner of her mouth. "Because I love you." He kissed her again.

Hildy furrowed her eyebrows in confusion. "How do you know?"

"Sweetheart, when I walked into that bedroom and saw you'd left with everything except the blanket I gave you, my whole world exploded. The thought of not having you in my life sucked the air out of my lungs. Now you're back in my arms, I can finally breathe. When you walked away from me all those years ago, you took a small piece of my heart with you. When you walked away from me this morning, you took the rest."

Guilt burned deep in her belly as she pondered his words. In her desperation to protect her own heart, it didn't occur to her she could be damaging Wil's. Hildy thought back through her day, finally understanding that constant ache in her chest was from leaving her heart behind with her blanket. Now the ache was gone, and she sure as fuck didn't want it to come back. Was that love? Maybe. "I don't want to sleep alone tonight."

HE HADN'T BLOWN IT, thank fuck. It was so hard to lay his heart on the line after she'd walked away. But he got it, she was scared, confused, and convinced he was going to leave her. After a lifetime of protecting herself, it was going to take time and a lot of testing before she was going to believe he was in it for the long haul. "I don't either."

"Can we sleep the way we did that first night, no blanket around me, just you?"

"If that's what you want."

"It's what I need."

"Okay, baby girl, you get yourself into bed. I'll join you as soon as I check the locks and brush my teeth." Wilson waited until Hildy was settled under the covers before he left the room.

With the house locked up tight and his teeth brushed, Wilson returned to the bedroom. Hildy had the covers pulled up to her ears and she was doing a laughable job of pretending to be asleep. She looked so adorable. He wanted to pounce on her and make her squirm. That would have to go on hold along with the ass-paddling she'd earned earlier. "Faker." Hildy's mouth twitched and Wilson chuckled. Damn, that felt good. He stripped to his boxers and slipped into bed beside Hildy. "Oh, you're naked."

Hildy giggled and placed her hand on Wil's bare belly before sliding it south. "Yeah, I am. The question is, why aren't you?"

He caught Hildy's wrist and pulled it away before she got near his erection. "No sex."

"But—"

"I need you to understand, really understand, I'm not here because I'm a selfish horny bastard and you're a great lay. I am here because I love you. All of you, exactly how you are. And until you trust me, there is no sex."

"I do trust you."

"No, you don't. But you will."

"What makes you think you know better than me whether I trust you?"

"Rope bondage. You want it as much as I do, but without absolute trust, it isn't going to happen."

"Seriously, I don't get sex until you get to tie me up?"

"Pretty much. Your trust is important to me. I can wait."

"What if I can't."

"Honey, nobody ever died from not having sex." Wilson slipped his arms around Hildy and shifted her until her back was pulled tight against his chest. She wiggled her ass into his groin and he almost reconsidered his no sex edict. "I love that you're feeling playful, baby, but you need to stop or I'm going to add to the punishment you've already earned tonight."

"Spoil sport."

Hildy finally stopped moving, and Wil concentrated on deflating his cock. He stroked her head and brushed his lips over her shoulder. "Hildy, what happened with your parents today?"

What the hell, she may as well tell him. He was still here, and it wasn't like it could get any worse. "They had discovered Uncle Erich left everything to me, and came to persuade me to rectify his error. When I said no, my mother resorted to more forceful methods."

"Baby, I'm so sorry I didn't protect you."

"Wil, I made my own choices and didn't give you any opportunity, so there's nothing to be sorry about."

"Okay, we'll agree to disagree. Your mother was the one who assaulted you?"

"Yeah. She was just getting started when my neighbour pulled into his driveway. I had enough of my wits about me to not let them come inside, so the minute a potential witness appeared, they legged it. I am fine, Wil. Honestly."

"I came over as soon as Sully called. He'd called to warn you, but it kept going straight to voice-mail. I assume you didn't check your messages."

"No, my phone is still off."

"New rule, baby girl, your phone stays on and you answer when a friend calls. No excuses."

"There you go, being all bossy again."

"Your safety is non-negotiable. You had a lot of people worried today."

He was right. She'd been inconsiderate. Guilt started to eat at her again.

"Stop beating yourself up, love."

Fuck, how did he always know?

"You give it away every time, and that's a good thing. For both of us. I would like to know one more thing. How come you snuck out instead of coming to me and using your safeword? You've used it before and it's been okay."

She'd asked herself the same question countless times already, and the answer was always the same. "I don't know."

"Okay. But don't be surprised if it has something to do with trust."

TEN

THE ROPE WAS rough in her hand. She felt guilty for going into Wil's toy bag, but she wanted to surprise him. She didn't think he really meant it when he said no sex, he was a man, after all. But as with everything else, he was true to his word.

Her face had been healed for almost two weeks and Wil hadn't so much as hinted at rope or bondage. He did occasionally pull out his Dom-voice which made her knees melt. She wondered if he realised she did stuff on purpose just to get him to use it. Probably.

She looked at the rope again. Not so scary. She thought about the photos Wil had of other women he'd tied up, and jealously reared its ugly green head. She didn't want him tying anyone up but her.

She checked the clock. Time to get moving, he'd be walking through the back door in a few minutes.

Naked, Hildy knelt at the door, her head bowed, Wil's rope in her outstretched arms. She was terrified this was going to backfire, but her patience had run out. She fought the urge to raise her head when the door opened, and she had a horrifying thought. What if Wil wasn't alone? Maybe she should have given this a little more careful thought.

"A naked woman bearing rope. What a beautiful sight to come home to. Up you get, sweetheart, it looks like we need to have a chat." Dom-voice.

Hildy lifted her head, relieved that Wil was alone and sporting a wide grin. He took the rope from her with one hand, and helped her up with the other. He pulled her into his arms and kissed her, teasing her lips open and plundering. Want surged through her like lightning through copper.

Wil took her hand and led her to the sofa in the living room. He laid the rope down, then pulled Hildy into his lap as he sat. "So, what's this all about?" He asked as he patted the rope beside him.

"Trust."

Wil hugged Hildy tight and kissed the top of her head. "Okay. First, show me your palms."

Yeah, that was fair. She held out her hands. Wil nodded, then lifted Hildy's hair and slowly worked his way around her hairline at the nape of her neck. He wouldn't find anything. She'd been so good. She hadn't ripped out any hair since that awful day.

"Such a good girl. Okay, we'll try something very basic, no knots. Stand up, lift your arms, and lace your fingers behind your head." Wil picked up the rope and folded it in half. "All I'm going to do is wrap this around you, just below your breasts and slip the two loose ends through the middle. Okay?"

Hildy looked at the rope Wil held out and nodded. He

stood behind her and reached around in front, lifting her boobs with his thumbs as he placed the rope right where her boobs and chest met. It felt a bit scratchy against her skin, but she liked it. How weird was that? The rope tightened briefly, then was gone.

"Good girl. That's enough for today."

"But—"

"Enough."

She spun around and put her hands on his chest. "Wil."

"Let's end this on a positive note. We can do more another time."

"Please?"

He took her face in his hands and touched his forehead to hers. "Baby, I'm so scared I'm going to fuck this up again, and I can't bear the thought of losing you."

Hildy clutched at his shirt, "Wil, I want this. I need this." He wrapped her in his arms and hugged her tight. She rested her head against his chest and she could hear his heart racing as she felt it pound against her cheek. Gradually it slowed and she felt him relax a little.

"Okay, we can try a rope harness, but I need you to promise me you'll safeword if you have a problem."

"I promise."

Wil released her and spun her around so her back was to him again. "Okay, we're going to start a little differently this time. Hands behind your head again, like you did before." Wil reached in front of her and placed the rope above her breasts and she felt a bit of friction at her back and some tugging as he tightened the rope "Give me a colour, love."

"Green."

"Good girl. Here comes the next one." He brought the rope around the front, this time beneath her breasts before she felt more friction and tugging. "Still green?"

God, she loved it. She didn't think she could get any greener. Each tug brought her a little more peace.

"I need an answer, love."

"Oh, yeah, I'm good."

"On we go, then." Another pass above her breasts, more tugging at the back, then he brought the rope over her shoulder and moved to stand in front of her. He grinned at her and she grinned back. He passed the rope between her breasts, slipping it beneath all the ropes that were around her chest. A little more fussing and tugging, then he placed the rope over her other shoulder. "Still good?"

"Mmm."

"I need a colour, love."

"Yeah, I'm green."

"Excellent. A knot at the back, and we're done." He stepped behind her and a few tugs later, he was done. "Still green, my good girl?"

"Hell, yeah."

"You look beautiful. Now go wait for me on the bed. On all fours, I think."

Hildy raced off. She didn't need to be told twice.

THE JANGLE of Wilson's belt buckle had Hildy wet and ready to beg. She'd waited weeks for this and she didn't want to wait another moment. She felt the bed shift behind her as Wil climbed on.

"I thought I wanted to fuck you like this, but I don't. I want to gaze into those beautiful eyes of yours while I love you. On your back, sweetheart."

Hildy turned over and her heart flipped in her chest. Wil's eyes smouldered as he stroked her cheek. He leaned down and touched his lips to hers before he kissed his way to her earlobe and nibbled. "I love you, Hildy Klein."

She wanted to say those words back so badly, but she was still trying to figure out what they meant. She needed to give him something, but it had to be something that meant the same to both of them. Then it came to her. "Wil?"

He pulled back and looked into her eyes, "Yes, love?"

"I...I trust you."

"Thank you, baby girl. That means everything to me." Wil crushed his lips to hers before trapping her bottom lip between his teeth and tugging gently. He caught hold of her wrists and held them over her head in one hand as he kneed her legs apart. He let go of her lip and kissed a trail south until he reached her nipple. He sucked and licked it as he slid one finger, then two into her eager pussy.

"Please."

He released her nipple with a pop. "Please what, love?"

"Please don't tease me."

"Okay. You've been such a good girl." He let go of her wrists and kneeled up. "Leave them there." He leaned over and grabbed a condom packet from the bedside table and opened it. He paused a moment. "On second thoughts, you do it."

Hildy grinned as she sat up and took the condom from him. Normally, she'd tease him for a bit, but she was done waiting. She deftly rolled the condom over his erection and flopped back on the bed throwing her arms back above her head

Wil positioned his cock at her entrance, holding it there as he leaned forward. He reached up and laced his fingers with hers, then rested his weight on his elbows. He lowered his mouth to hers as he slowly entered her body.

Fuck, she didn't want slow and gentle. She was horny as hell and wanted hard and fast. He eased out of her, and as he slid back, in she thrust her hips up to meet his. "That wasn't quite what I had in mind, but we can go there." He let go of her hands and rolled them over until she was on top.

Hildy knew Wil wasn't likely to give her control very often, so she'd have to make every opportunity count. She laced her fingers with his, like he'd done earlier and lifted up so just the head of his cock was inside. She kissed him as she slid down hard, taking him deep. She rocked back and forth for a few strokes before rising up and plunging down again. She varied her depth and speed until she felt the tell-tale flutter. She plunged deep one more time and ground her clit into Wil's pubic bone. She let go of his hands and guided them to her hips. He pushed up into her as he held her tight against his body, the friction doing delicious things until she finally let go with a long, low moan.

Wilson held her hips tighter and thrust up and ground into her, sending her over once more before she felt his cock pulsate as he came. Spent, she lowered herself onto his chest and his voice rumbled. "A quick cuddle now, then it's off with the condom and the harness." She nodded and drifted off, only vaguely aware of Wil untying her.

ELEVEN

HILDY JOINED Mac in the kitchen where she was busy loading the dishwasher. "So, you're really going to give up your place and move in here with Finn?"

"Yup. It's still months away, but it's only a formality."

"Still a pretty serious formality."

"It's not marriage."

"Close enough."

"Brat."

"You love me anyway."

"I do. So, are you really up for this?"

"Yeah, I am."

Mac closed the dishwasher and turned to Hildy. "Safeword if you need to."

"I know, but I'm relaxed." Hildy held out her palms. "See, no nail marks and here," She lifted her hair, "no pulling."

"In that case, let's go. Finn's been vibrating with anticipation all day."

"Ha, so has Wil."

Hildy and Mac sauntered down to the play room where Finn and Wilson sat on chairs side by side.

Finn grinned. "Glad to see you both finally made it. We are beginning to think you weren't coming. Mac, strip and bend over, please."

Mac walked over to Finn, slipped out of her clothes and folded them, then bent forward resting her palms flat on the floor.

"Good girl" Finn picked up a butt plug off the table next to him and loaded it with lube. Mac moaned as the plug slid home.

"Oh, you like that, do you, baby girl?"

Hildy swivelled her head toward Wil. She'd been so absorbed in what she was watching, the soft whisper caught her off guard. "What?"

"You tend to pay very close attention whenever Finn plugs Mac's ass and that little smile that plays over your lips gives you away. Mac's getting a fun spanking tonight, but your ass still has to pay for putting yourself down while you were injured, so we'll be doing a bit of a variation on Mac and Finn's scene."

Shivers shot down Hildy's spine, and oh boy, they were the good kind. She smiled up at Wilson and he couldn't quite keep his lips from tipping up at the corners. "Okay."

"Strip, fold your clothes, and lay over my lap exactly like Mac."

As she removed and folded her clothes, Hildy studied Mac's position over Finn's lap. Her hips were against Finn's left thigh, her own legs extended back and trapped beneath Finn's right leg. Her toes supported her, bent almost like she was wearing high heel shoes, and her palms were flat on the floor. Okay, it looked precarious, but she could do that.

Hildy laid herself over Wil's lap, emulating Mac as best she could. Once she'd settled, Wil clamped his leg over hers. He stroked her back and she relaxed.

"Good girl. You earned ten with the leather strap for putting yourself down. I know you thought I wouldn't follow through, so I decided to give you a little added intensity to make sure you get the message loud and clear."

He parted her buttocks and she felt a little thrill. He was finally going to use a butt plug. She liked anal, but Wil was taking everything so damned carefully, they'd barely got past missionary since they'd started having sex again.

The probing at her anus didn't feel like much more than a cold wet finger. Okay, maybe a bit bigger than a finger, but not by much. It felt pretty good, though. Hildy moaned a little, then Wil wiggled the plug a bit before pulling it most of the way out and pushing it back in. Then the burning started. "Ow, take it out, my asshole is on fire."

"Excellent, now you're ready for your spanking. I'm feeling generous, so I'll make it quick."

Hildy looked over at Mac who smiled and winked while Finn smacked and rubbed her ass. That didn't look so— Holy shit! The burn in her asshole was barely a glow compared to the hell Wil rained on her ass. By the time she had her breath back, the blows stopped, the plug was out, and Wil was stroking her back.

"All done, love, clean slate."

Hildy panted through the waves pain "That hurt."

"It was meant to. I warned you not to say or think bad things about yourself, and I shouldn't have let you get away with it as much as I did. No more. From now on, I have a zero tolerance policy for that shit, and I'll be increasing the consequences with each infraction."

"I didn't think you'd be that mean about it."

"Now you know." Wil opened his legs and caught Hildy under the arms to help her up. "There you go. Are you ready for some fun, feel good stuff now?"

They'd talked in detail about the plans for the evening. She'd been letting Wil tie her up for weeks now and she loved it. She'd even got to the point where she could ask Wil to tie her in a rope harness when she needed to feel snug. Tonight, Wil and Finn were going to tie her and Mac together and play. She couldn't wait.

She cupped his face and kissed him. "I trust you. I'm ready for anything."

One Gold Triquetra (Dominant Cord, Book 3)

A decade ago, a bad play-date turned composer Ella Hudson off BDSM.

Now she's been offered a performance opportunity too good to pass up, but it means working closely with Jackson and Griffin--world class musicians, lovers, and Doms intent on adding her to their relationship.

While Ella struggles to deny her true desires, maintaining her vanilla facade becomes increasingly difficult as the men re-introduce her to a world she'd written off.

ONE GOLD TRIQUETRA

PROLOGUE

JACK SET his toy bag down with far more care than his temper demanded. "Dammit, Griff, I thought this one had promise."

"I know, babe." Griff leaned in and touched his forehead to Jack's. "Look, do you really think we need a beard? Sully knows the score and he's cool with it. Do you honestly think Wil and Finn will care? I'm fucking tired of sneaking around. You like to fuck me, I like to fuck you. So what? It's nobody's business but ours, and I don't like constantly having to produce a third to camouflage our relationship. Don't get me wrong, I'm always happy to have some subbie pussy around to torture and fuck, but not to keep up appearances. It makes me feel like I'm not good enough."

Jack brushed a gentle kiss over Griff's lips. "Idiot. You know it's more than just fucking. I love you. You're way beyond good enough; you're everything to me. However, the reality is, neither of us subs, so even if we outed ourselves, we would still need a submissive if we wanted to play at Finn's parties."

"You're right, but I'm fed up with playing musical subbies. This one seemed like she might work out, you know? I don't understand how I could have been so blind."

"Don't go taking all the credit. I was just as blind. She took everything we dished out and begged for more. Maybe I was more wilfully ignorant than blind. Can you imagine how deeply we could have got involved with her if that business with Hildy hadn't happened tonight? All the trouble she could have caused for us? I feel queasy just thinking about it."

"We sure dodged a bullet with that one. Speaking of Hildy, what's the deal? Wil is notorious for going out of his way to avoid newbies, yet he shows up to a play party with one?"

"Not our business."

"I know, but I don't think we've ever had a newbie at a party before. Even Mac had some previous experience."

"Again, not our business."

"You're no fun."

Jack grabbed the hem of Griff's shirt and lifted. "Oh baby, I'm lots of fun."

CHAPTER ONE

Griff smiled wide as he followed Jack into Finn's music room. "Sully, you old slacker, it's about fucking time you got back to work."

"I figured if I didn't show soon, I'd be looking for a new gig."

"Does this mean you're back in full swing?"

"I don't know about full swing, but I've been swizzling the hitty-sticks a little. Fucking busted ribs completely crimped my style."

Griff just about swallowed his tongue when Mac walked in wearing nothing but clover clamps on her nipples and leather cuffs on her wrists. His head was full of questions, but when Jack caught his eye, he nodded and kept them to himself. Not his business.

Sully, who considered everything his business, was not so polite. "Nice outfit, sweetie. Special occasion?" Mac glared at Sully and slowly flipped him the finger.

Griff held back a chuckle when he spotted Finn leaning against the door jamb. Oh, for a bowl of popcorn.

"Oh dear. What an unfortunate turn of events, my love." Finn walked across the room, sat in his chair, and patted his hands on his thighs. Mac stalked over to him and laid herself across his lap.

He reached down and grabbed the thin wooden cleaning rod for his flute. "Before we begin, why are you being punished?"

"I was disrespectful."

"Yes, you were. I accept that you and Sully have a special understanding, but when I have your submission, you must be respectful to everyone, regardless of your normal dynamic. It's not like you don't know any better. We've had this same conversation before. What was your punishment last time?"

"Ten strokes with your hand."

"And what happens with repeat offences?"

"Double the last with whatever implement you choose."

"That means it'll be twenty with the cleaning rod. Colour, Mac?"

"I'm green."

"Good enough. I'll keep count. Do not move." Finn placed his left hand on the small of Mac's back before taking the first stroke. He laid stripe after stripe across her ass, never striking the same spot twice. Mac's facial contortions and tears were the only sign of her struggle to accept her punishment. By the time Finn was done, her ass was striped like a candy cane. "All done, love. Now go apologise to Sully, and once your slate is clean, we will continue with what you were supposed to be doing before this little interlude."

Mac rose from Finn's lap and accepted the tissue he

held out. She took a moment to wipe her tears and blow her nose. Then she went over to Sully, knelt at his feet, and rested her forehead on his knees. "I'm sorry."

"All is forgiven, sweetie. I'm sorry too. I shouldn't have teased you." Sully leaned forward and kissed her head. Mac looked up and smiled, then rose to her feet and returned to Finn.

"Good girl. Hands behind your back and turn around." As soon as her back was turned, Finn clipped her cuffs together and kissed her shoulder. "Off you go, sweetheart."

Griff caught Sully's eye and raised an eyebrow as Mac sat on the piano bench. Sully shrugged and shook his head slightly. How the hell were they supposed to have a productive rehearsal with a naked, decorated Mac in the room? More to the point, how was Finn going to concentrate on the music when most of his focus would be on his sub who would be teetering on the edge of her limits?

"Holy shit, if I'd known it was bring your sub to work day, I would have brought Hildy. She and Mac would look so cute sitting on the piano bench with their tits clamped togeth—"

The colour drained from Mac's face, and Finn flew to her side as he snapped at Wilson. "Enough." He unclipped Mac's cuffs and gathered her into his arms. "Sweetie, I fucked up. I'm so sorry." As he left the room with Mac, Finn turned to the rest of the group and said, "You guys go ahead without me."

Wilson stepped towards them. "Mac, Finn, I'm—"

"Not right now, Wil. I need to take care of her. Maybe before you leave..."

Wilson ran his hand through his hair. "Yeah, sure."

As soon as Finn and Mac were gone, Sully pounced. "Dammit, Wil. What were you thinking?"

"I wasn't. It just slipped out. What was going on, anyway?"

"My best guess is Finn was pushing at Mac's issue with the piano bench and figured doing it during rehearsal with a room full of Doms was the best way to do it. He probably would have been right if he'd thought to give us a heads up. He's usually more on the ball about this kind of thing."

Taking pity on Wil, Griff spoke up. "Don't beat yourself up about it, Sully was rather indelicate himself and Mac's reaction earned her a candy-striped ass."

Sully had the decency to look a little sheepish. "Yeah, I think Griff and Jack are the only ones who haven't caused Mac pain of one kind or another today. Right, I guess we should get on with it. What are we playing first?"

One Gold Heart (Dominant Cord, Book 1)

Finn Taylor is an asshole. So why does he keep showing up in Mac's late-night fantasies as the Dom of her dreams? She can't even ignore him, because she's stuck working with the fellow musician for the Christmas concert season.

Mac Wallis is a mess, and Finn can't fall for a submissive who's so damaged she needs medication just to get through a performance. But he's drawn to the beautiful oboist, even as he keeps pissing her off. He can't resist trying to take care of her--in every way.

Tainted Pearl: A Rock Star Prequel

Lust at first sight has never been a problem for Doug Fraser before, but something about Biddy O'Mara screams "hands off". Except the private, mysterious musician is also the sexiest, most captivating woman he's ever crammed into close quarters with.

Biddy can't afford any distractions while on a month long eco-activism island adventure. The rock star is incognito for a very good cause, but the irresistible camera operator quickly proves a big, bad complication.

A fling is inevitable. But Doug's not relationship material, and the more he gets to know Biddy, the more he realizes she's the type of girl you take home to meet your mother—even if you don't know all her secrets.

Tainted Shadow (Tainted Pearl, Book 1)

Tainted Pearl's lead singer has a stalker problem and bodyguard Brody Clarke doesn't think twice about cutting his vacation short when he's asked to protect her.

Sparks fly—and not the good kind—when he rubs the rabidly independent rock star the wrong way. Now he needs to convince her that letting him be in control might just save her life.

And if it has the side benefit of turning those sparks into a completely different kind of heat? Brody's up for that kind of dominance as well.

Prime Minster (Frisky Beavers #1)

Gavin:

Ellie Montague is smart, sensitive, and so gorgeous it hurts to look at her. She's also an intern in my office. The office of the Prime Minister of Canada.*

That's me. The PM.

She calls me that because when she calls me Sir, I get hard and she gets flustered, and as long as she's my intern, I can't twist my hands in her strawberry-blonde hair and show her what else I'd like her to do with that pretty pink mouth.**

Ellie:

How much I like the PM varies on a daily basis. He's intense, controlling, and a perfectionist in every way—and he demands the same of his staff.

How much I want him never wavers.

There's something about him that tugs at me deep inside, and makes me wish that just once he'd cross the line in a late night work session. I'd take that secret to the grave if it meant I got a taste of the barely restrained beast inside him.***

FOOTNOTES:

* This is a fictional erotic romance. No prime ministers or interns were harmed in the making of this book.

** Except it's a BDSM romance, so they were hurt a little.

*** Spoiler alert: she gets more than a taste. And she likes it.

ACKNOWLEDGMENTS

Élianne Adams, Elizabeth Varlet, and Zoe York for their unwavering support and encouragement. The wonderful gang of Divas who are generous in so many ways. And of course, my wonderful, supportive husband, who says yes to almost everything...except another dog.

Surrounded by mist-covered mountains, Sadie Haller lives a quiet life with her husband and fur-babies.

Where to find Sadie

sadiehaller.com
sadie@sadiehaller.com